# THE MIRRORED BOX

## ANGELIQUE MANON

L.R. Price Publications Ltd

Copyright © 2016 L.R. Price Publications Ltd
Published 2016 by

L.R. Price Publications Ltd,
27 Old Gloucester Street,
London, WC1N 3AX.
www.lrpricepublications.com
ISBN: 0992903742
ISBN-13: 9780992903749

# THE MIRRORED BOX

---

## ANGELIQUE MANON

## CHAPTER ONE

There was pain, there was blood.

Is that all? Is that it? There is just pain? Where is that fantastic feeling they are always writing about? All these books I had read about passionate love and romance, I wondered if they were all just a dreamed-up fantasy.

Damien was a doctor and twelve years older than me - I was seventeen. We had been in a relationship for six months already, when he asked me to meet him in his room at the hospital.

I had been sat on the bed, waiting for him to come back. Whilst I waited I stared at his pet bird - a canary - which he kept in a small cage.

When he opened the door he looked at me, then at the cage, and moved it to the window, so that the bird could enjoy the last rays of light.

'What a lovely gesture,' I thought.

He did not say a word, but instead smiled at me. He removed his white shoes and his white socks.

I admired his figure. He was a very strong man, well over six feet tall, with a fine chiselled face, light blond, very wavy hair and dark blue eyes. Extremely confident and proud, he knew that everybody noticed him when he entered a room.

"Why are you taking off your shoes and socks?" I asked.

He didn't reply, but walked across the room and closed the curtains. It was almost dark, and the canary stopped singing.

He stood in front of me and took off his white shirt and his white pants. It dawned on me what he was doing. It never would have occurred to him to ask me what I thought.

I started to shiver - I didn't know whether I was cold or nervous, but I was glad there was no light.

I just looked at his towering figure and froze.

He removed my dress and my shoes - he did not remove my bra.

He pushed me backwards, down on the bed and crawled on top of me. I wanted to kiss him and tried to embrace him with my arms.

He did not want that.

He grabbed both my wrists with one hand,

pinned them above my head, and removed my knickers with his other hand.

Then his hand slid under my underwear. His one hand felt like many, as his fingers pushed inside me.

Then he used his knees to force my legs open.

I felt his erection against me.

I wasn't aroused and dreaded what was coming.

He just thrust into me.

Hard.

His penis felt like scissors had just cut me - the pain was excruciating.

I knew it was my fault: I was too small for him.

I cringed, weary and pensive when he lay on me. He was very heavy. I couldn't breathe.

He thrust inside me again and continued to thrust into me, each time deeper and deeper.

I tried to get away – but then it was over.

He released my wrists and kissed my face.

I began to cry.

He pressed me close to his body and lifted me up like a little doll; "I will love you forever and ever."

Yes, that first night with a man is a night no woman will forget.

ANGELIQUE MANON

## CHAPTER TWO

Dreaming is easy when you live in the natural paradise of the South of France.

Today, as I lay on the beach enjoying the Mediterranean sun, it was my wedding to Damien that I dreamed of.

It had been over a year since that first night with Damien and we were now engaged, due to be married in only three months, after my eighteenth birthday.

I loved Damien, I loved my family and I loved my job.

My father was a doctor as well, and having completed my associate's degree for medical assistants, I began to work for my Dad, running his busy office.

As the sun began to set, I packed up my belongings and returned home.

When I entered the living room, I noticed the silence. This was unusual, since the house was always full of classical music.

My mother and father were sat there,

looking at me with an expression on their faces that I had not seen since my grandpa had passed away.

"Sit down, Angelique," said my father.

I sat.

My father went and got a bottle of wine and three glasses.

"I have been to see Damien," said my father.

"Why didn't I come with you," I said, "I would have loved to see you at work, to listen and learn."

"Because this is not a work matter - this is a personal matter, and some matters must remain confidential, and be dealt with between man and man."

I was confused.

My father filled three glasses and placed one in front of me. He opened his cigar case, lit the cigar and placed it immediately into the ashtray. Then he took my hand, looked at me and very quietly, almost whispered: "There will be no wedding, Angelique."

I looked at him, and then looked at my mother. She sat there with a face devoid of any expression - her eyes were rigid; she looked like a statue made of stone.

"What happened?!" I cried out. "You just came back from visiting Damien? Is he ill? What on Earth happened?"

"No, he is not ill, Angelique, but he had to make a medical decision, and for medical reasons he decided that he cannot go through with the wedding."

"What medical decision?!" I shouted. "He is perfectly healthy - what happened to him?"

"It is not him," said my father; "it is you."

"Me? There is nothing wrong with me," I whimpered. "What is wrong with me?"

My mother got up and went into the bathroom.

I heard her vomit.

"Look, Angelique," said my father very slowly, and he pronounced every word so carefully, as if he was talking to fool: "We are both doctors, and it is only ethical that we tell each other the truth - Damien is a doctor, Damien's father and mother are doctors. I had to tell him that the chances are that you can't bear a healthy child."

"What are you talking about, Father?"

"It's genetic. There is a genetic illness in your mother's family: she has a brother who is very sick. The gene that impedes him may have been passed to you. You may never have children, and if you do, the child will be very sick. So, you see: you can't have children."

7

I felt like I had been winded. I shook my head and began to cry. "Damien will marry me," I said. "And I know it beyond the shadow of a doubt. We have not had a single fight - he adores me. I am a medical assistant - I have learned all I need to know with you, Dad, to help him in his new office. He will never marry another woman. We belong to each other - we are the perfect match, and I will see him now."

"You will not see him now," said my father. "He is not at the hospital."

"I will phone him then."

"You won't reach him, Angelique."

My body began to shake, and when I picked up the glass of wine, my hands shook so terribly that I spilled the wine all over the table.

"Come with me," said my mother. "Come with me and we will go to bed. We will talk tomorrow."

It was inconceivable to say no to either my mother or my father. I had never said no, and my sisters had never said no. In my entire life, I had never seen my parents argue. My father made the decisions, and my mother abided by all the decisions.

She took my hand, and we walked upstairs to my room. She watched me undress. She had a glass of water in her hand with some tablets, which she held as tears ran down her cheeks.

"There are things in this world, my darling, that are difficult to understand," she said, "but I will explain them to you very carefully. When you are my age, you will understand. Right now it is very painful. Remember that we women are in this world to have children. We are in this world to care for our husbands - this is our life. I will help you, my darling. Take these tablets and go to sleep."

I swallowed the tablets, as my father entered the room.

"You know how much I love you," he said, "and you know how proud I am that you have been such a good student all your life. My own life is full of sunshine because you work with me. I do not want you to suffer. I will give you something so that you can sleep."

He gave me an injection in my arm, and I woke up sixteen hours later.

My calmness surprised me - I was collected, not drowsy. There was stillness in me - placidity. He must have tranquilized me - I felt peace and serenity, quietness within myself. Nobody was in the house, and both cars were gone.

I called Damien, first at the hospital, then at his apartment - no answer.

I called his sister - she had not heard anything.

I took his spare key and got a taxi to his apartment.

His car was there, so I walked up the front stairs and let myself in.

He sat in the living room, unshaven, with a whisky bottle in front of him and cigarettes all around. He never smoked, and I hardly ever saw him drink.

I knelt in front of him. I put my arms around his legs and looked into his face.

"Damien, it's not true, is it? I mean, it could not possibly be... right?"

He bit his lips - first his upper lip and then his lower lip. He looked at me.

"So, you are discarding me? You're throwing me away three months before our wedding? There has never been an issue or any discontent between the two of us."

"I wanted children," he said.

"We can have children, and if you are afraid, we can adopt some. Our life is more important."

"I have been thinking about this all night, Angelique - I have not had a second of sleep. But I am a doctor, and I know the ramifications. I want my own children."

"So I am abandoned - cast off? I am only

worth something if I can bear children? My love to you means nothing because there are a million women you can have - women with good genes. Is this correct?"

"Don't use this word 'discarded', Angelique - it sounds pathetic. A woman lives and is born to have children. A woman exists to be a mother. You can never be, in fact you *should* never be, a mother. Is that the advice I can give you?"

"I have loved you more than I ever loved anyone in my life."

I left his apartment. I did not cry. I was not upset. I felt nothing but hatred.

'I will never love a man so long as I live,' I said to myself. 'I don't need them, I despise them, and they make me nauseous. I detest them, and I hate them.'

I even hated the weakness of my mother: she did not fight for me. She knew exactly what Dad intended to do. She could have prevented it, but she did not. Nobody cared for me. They destroyed my life, and they would never see me again. Never.

I bit my teeth together until it hurt and went home by taxi.

The house was empty.

I took the two largest suitcases I could find.

11

I packed them with my passport, my birth certificate, my driver's license, my medical assistant's diploma, my nicest clothes and shoes. It took no more than an hour before I was done.

Then, I wandered through the house and selected a picture of the whole family: grandma, grandpa, my sisters, Mum and Dad, and took an individual picture of my brother.

I wrote on a large piece of paper: "I am in Paris. Will call." Then I left.

## CHAPTER THREE

I had no idea where I would go, but told the taxi driver to head to the airport - I would make my mind up on the way there. I thought back to when I was sixteen, when I had had a pen pal in America - for years we wrote to each other.

Corresponding in a foreign language was the "in" thing to do - our parents promoted it, and our schoolteachers told us that it was a splendid idea. It was so exciting to receive a letter from America. It lasted for almost three years.

We exchanged pictures, and we called each other. Our relationship had slowly turned sexual over the phone, even though we were continents away from each other.

"What does sex feel like, Stephen?" I had asked. I just could not imagine it. My fantasy was a wild dream that could never happen, and it involved intimacies with a perfect imaginary lover.

"What do you think it feels like when I use

my mouth, my lips, and my tongue and kiss the regions around your nipples?" he answered.

I felt blood rushing through me. This was so new, so exciting. I never would have dared ask anybody but Stephen a question like that.

"I will be pleasing you with my tongue Angelique," he continued, "I will caress your ears with my lips, I will be cupping your breasts with my hands and very carefully stroke your inner thighs."

My whole body tingled as he spoke. "What does an orgasm feel like for you, Stephen?" I asked.

There was silence, then he said: "My head begins to spin, my body starts shaking. Have you seen the volcano erupt in Italy, Angelique?"

"Yes."

"That is what an orgasm is like," he said.

'Geez,' I thought: 'it must be amazing.'

"What does an orgasm feel like for you, Angelique?"

"I don't know, Stephen."

"Put your hand between your legs, Angelique. Touch yourself. Tell me what it feels like for you."

This was the first time I had masturbated. The fact that it was for Stephen felt special to me.

He told me he wanted to make love to me in

so many different positions. I didn't even know what he was talking about, but it sounded wonderful.

When I met Damien and wrote that I was engaged, he stopped, and never wrote to me again.

But we were friends, and right now he is my only friend in this world.

When I arrived at the airport I had made my mind up: 'I will go to America and I will call Stephen. He will help me.' But, first I knew I would need a visa, and the only place I could get one was the American Embassy.

So, after I paid the taxi driver, I went into the airport and booked a ticket for the next flight to Paris.

## CHAPTER FOUR

When I landed in Paris I called my sister from the airport.

"Angelique!" she yelled. "What are you doing in Paris? Listen to me - you never listen. You are driving the parents insane. What is wrong with you?"

"I will always be in contact with them," I said, very composed; "not a week will go by when I will not try to write, and I will call you frequently. My life in Nice is over - I will not return. Tell them I love them forever. Tell them I am grateful for the years they have cared for me. Tell them I need to find my own way."

'I am eighteen years old,' I thought; 'I have been to Paris once before and I know it like the palm of my hand.

'I will go to Montmartre, and I will lose myself again in the steep and cobbled streets. I will go to the *Basilica de Sacre-Coeur*, the fantastic white church that sits on the crest of the hill.

'Then I will ask God at the Basilica why

Damien has dumped me. I will probably not get an answer, and so I will never go to church again.'

I spent my first night in Paris in a very nice hotel. It was like being at home - I was well looked after. But, when I looked at the money I had, I realised this place was too expensive and would kill me financially.

After leaving the hotel I found a second-hand book store and went in: I would need some company, otherwise I would get lonely or bored. I purchased two books: *"Bonjour Tristesse"* by Françoise Sagan and *"The Woman Destroyed"* by Simone de Beauvoir. I felt like the characters in the pages: women who had been trampled on and kicked to the ground. It would make me feel so much better to read these books.

I continued to wander around and found a flea market, where I purchased a little portable radio - this would also keep me company, I thought.

Paris was nothing like I remembered. I kept getting lost and I still hadn't found a single room that I could afford.

By the end of the second day I started to get scared: I thought that I would run out of money and have to live and sleep on the street.

I went to a shop bought a pack of cigarettes, a small bottle of gin, and several bottles of tonic water. I had never smoked nor desired hard liquor, but I figured it would probably make me feel better.

On the way back to the hotel, carrying my bags, I saw an antique shop with a huge beautiful mirror in the window - it caught my attention.

Next to it was a tatty door, with a sign that must have been there for a while, because the rain had washed away the letters. It read: *"Room to rent"*.

I knocked.

A tiny old woman opened the door. She smiled at me with this huge smile, and had not one tooth in her mouth. She wore some old baggy pants with a large jumper, and she looked about eighty years old.

"Come on in, my little darling," she said; "come on in - I have a wonderful, comfortable room for you."

She pulled me by my skirt, grabbing it with her hand, so I had to follow her.

"Sit down here," she said and gave me a

little push.

I almost fell onto the large sofa behind me.

Before she could go any further, I said quickly: "Do you have a shower?"

"You need a shower?"

"Yes."

"You need a shower every day?"

"Yes, every day."

"This is a strange habit!" she chuckled. "I have no shower, but you could use my basement, where I do the laundry."

"Show me," I said.

She got up and grabbed me by the skirt again. By now I wondered if she needed to hold on to something, and I let her drag me down the stairs, into a very dark basement.

The room had a cement floor, one tiny window where I could see the shoes of people walking on the street, a light bulb hanging from the ceiling, a large table, and an iron on an ironing board. On the floor were two large washbasins, obviously for laundry.

"Take the hose," she said: "you see?"

She took a rubber hose and attached it to the sink in the laundry basin, opened the water, and out came big stream of water. It ran onto the cement floor, right into a little hole in the corner.

She kept on laughing, and when she did her

mouth would grow so large it looked like a hole in her head.

She was warm and friendly and I liked her.

"How can I close the door and make sure nobody shows up when I take the hose?" I asked her.

"Nobody will show up – it's *my* laundry room," she smiled. "But, take the table and move it in front of the door if you are worried."

She grabbed my skirt again.

"Why don't you take my hand?" I said, and took her hand in mine.

"Oh, this is nice - very nice," she said, and she gripped my hand with an amazing strength.

I realised that she needed me to walk, or to see.

We walked back up into her living room.

The room to rent was very small, but it had a nice window. It had a bed that looked like a futon, an old tall, deep cupboard, a table, a chair, a lamp, a beer glass on the table and an ashtray. A large, blue, ceramic dish and a ceramic milk can were on the floor.

"Thank you, I'll take it," I said.

"I want a month's rent now," she smiled.

"Can you give me a receipt to show that I paid you the rent?" I said.

"You are a strange little girl. First you want a

shower every day, then you want a receipt. What is wrong with you? Or perhaps you don't you trust me?"

"Oh, I trust you, and I like you, and I like your house very much," I laughed, "but I need you to write me a receipt, and I need a key to the front door."

"Very well," she grinned.

I took her hand before she could grab me by the skirt again.

We walked into her kitchen. She sat down at a table, and I noticed that other than a stove, a sink and some cupboards, there was nothing in the kitchen, not even a refrigerator.

"Where is your food?" I asked.

"In my cold storage room," she said proudly, and took out a piece of paper and a pen. "And what is your name?"

"Angelique."

"What a beautiful name," she said, and then with large letters, she wrote: "Angelique has paid one month's rent." She signed it, and gave it to me.

I gave her the money.

"I will be back within an hour with all my things," I said.

"Thank you. A miracle… oh, a miracle…" she exclaimed.

"A miracle?" I asked.

"I am sorry," she said; "I am almost blind, and I have been trying to rent this room for such a long time - I prayed to God every day. I cannot manage on my own. I even wondered if I would die alone in here and no-one would ever know. But you are here now, Angelique. You are an angel, and God is good."

I was stunned by what she said.

She handed me the key and I went to inspect my room - the key worked perfectly when I returned with my luggage. Everything was clean and the linen even smelled good.

I had only eaten a sandwich at noon but I was not hungry. I opened up the gin bottle and took the beer glass, which stood on the night table - I filled it with half gin and half tonic. Then I opened the cigarettes and started to smoke - they made me cough like hell. The drink tasted extremely strong, but very good. But the half-glass of gin and tonic had a devastating effect, probably because I had an empty stomach: when I got up from the futon, I almost fell onto the floor. I poured a second drink and smoked a second cigarette.

The cigarettes and the gin were horrible. Just like making love: it takes some time to appreciate and enjoy.

On my third day in Paris, I learned what a hangover was.

## CHAPTER FIVE

By the fifth day I had a job as a waitress at a bar.

When I met the owner, he told me: "You can eat as much as you want. You can choose your dinner from the menu, and you can eat in the staffroom. You can never drink liquor-water - juices are all you are allowed to have. You will have two fifteen-minute breaks, and you have an hour for dinner. You can start today."

He gave me a cute uniform that fit me like a glove.

The time I worked in this bar indoctrinated me into the world of men, a world I had only previously experienced with Damien. I met them sober, and I observed them drunk. I realised that they generally did not value women: they were interested only in beauty and sex; all ages, professions, good-looking or ugly, fat or slim, rich or poor, old or young - once they had consumed a certain amount of liquor, their real personalities came out. A stunning, good-looking man, educated and professional in his demeanour, could turn into a vicious animal with an appalling vocabulary.

They slapped my behind, they squeezed my breasts, they got up and tried to kiss me, they slipped their hands under my skirt and tried to feel me, and they tried to pull down my knickers.

The owner would always shout and swear at the customers that did this, and get rid of them. I was never hurt, and the tips I received were very generous, but this did not make up for the violation that I felt.

Every week I mailed a postcard, telling my parents how happy I was. I did not phone my sister any more, because my mum picked up the phone twice and I could not stand hearing her cry.

"Listen to me, Angelique," she cried; "listen - you never listen! Dad figured we could work things out with Damien."

"But Damien was not interested, right?"

There was silence.

I said quickly: "I love you, Mum," and hung up.

I remembered my original plan of going to America, and realised I could not stay in Paris.

So, I went to the American Embassy. The lady there told me that I would receive my green card quickly if I could come up with a sponsor.

I called Stephen, my pen pal.

It had been two years since we spoke. I had last spoken to him when I was engaged, but despite my engagement, I was sure I had a friend for the rest of my life.

"What are you doing in Paris?" he immediately asked.

"I ran away from home."

"What? Why? Have you had a fight with Damien?"

"He doesn't want me."

"Come on, Angelique – don't give me that bullshit."

"It's true. Can you sponsor me? I need a sponsor to come to America."

"Is this a joke?"

"No, of course not."

"You must be kidding. This means a financial obligation. Are you crazy?"

"Stephen, please. I will earn money, and I will be successful - I can speak three languages. I will never be a burden - I will pay you back. Please, for goodness sake, please help me."

"I'm married and I have children," he said flatly. "Sponsoring is out of the question.

However, I will help you once you are in America."

"But Stephen… Wait… what? You have children?"

"Yes, I have a family."

"My God, we only stopped writing to each other two years ago. I don't understand."

"I had children then." His voice was cold and detached.

I felt sick.

"So you are probably ten or twenty years older than I am? And our love for each other meant nothing? You lied about your age? You lied about everything?"

"I did not lie about everything, Angelique: if I was there I would still fuck you."

"God, you're sick! Stop! All you can think about is sex!" I shouted. "Are you still in sales? Do you still have the house, the car and ..." I started to cry.

"It doesn't matter what I have, what I do not have, or what I do. I will help you, I promise, once you are in America, but I will not sponsor you. Okay?"

"Okay, Stephen. Thank you for absolutely nothing."

I slammed the phone down.

I went home, threw myself onto the futon

and wept.

Three years, and my only friend in this world was gone... gone! Thank God I had destroyed all those letters. Thank God my parents had never seen the letters.

'You bastard,' I thought; 'You lousy, miserable bastard! I don't need you, but when I see you - and I *will* meet you, one of these days - I will make sure that you get what you deserve. I hate men, I hate *all* men.'

Then I remembered someone had told me about Canada. It was said to be idyllic, with plenty of work and opportunity.

I will go to Canada instead.

The next day I went to the Canadian Embassy - the staff there were fantastic.

"We need people with your background. Go to Quebec - you will get a job immediately."

I had not felt wanted for so long, I knew that I had made the right decision.

It took almost three months before I obtained my visa and booked my flight for Canada.

When I told my landlady that I was going to leave to go to Canada, all she did was smile and squeeze my hands.

That night, when I was in bed, she came to

my room.

There was a knock at my door, and when I opened it she was stood there, wearing the same clothes, but with bare feet.

She stretched her hands out and yelled: "Angelique, look at me!"

Every fingernail and toenail was painted a different colour. I could not help but laugh.

She came into my room with a bottle of rum and began dancing, before falling onto my futon.

The next day she collapsed, and I had to call an ambulance came to pick her up.

I visited her in the hospital every day after I finished work.

On my last scheduled day in Paris I was absolutely shocked: I went to the hospital and a nurse told me that my landlady had passed away in the night.

## CHAPTER SIX

When I arrived in Canada I felt like my new life had begun.

The first place I stayed in was Montreal - it was an experience. Even though I spoke French, which was my native tongue, the French spoken there was so different. They understood me when I spoke slowly, but I hardly understood them. I had not expected that, and I had to ask again and again: "And what did you say?"

At first I had a great time - I spent my days in the cinema, watching one movie after another, drinking Coke, eating popcorn and smoking cigarettes. In France, you could only watch one movie with one ticket, not like Canada.

Despite this, I felt terribly alone in Montreal, so I took a train to Toronto.

In Toronto, they spoke English, and since I had learned English at school, I knew enough to easily get by and speak to people.

I had learnt my lesson from Paris, and found a cheap hotel to stay in, whilst I got my bearings.

I began immediately applying for jobs so that I could sustain myself - any job would be fine. I saw an ad in the paper: *"Assembly line workers wanted".*

I walked into the personnel office at the factory and a very friendly woman, about forty years of age, asked me to sit down.

"My name is June Brown," she said in English, and reached across her desk to shake my hand. "I gather you are applying for the assembly line worker's job?"

I just nodded my head.

"Do you speak English?" she asked.

"Yes, I'm just nervous."

She smiled; "Where are you from?"

"Paris, France," I replied, and handed her my papers: my landed immigration papers, my passport, and my other certificates.

She placed them on her desk without even looking at them, and pulled out a large book.

"I love Paris, although I have never been - I have seen it in pictures," she said. "You will get on fine here. We pay one-hundred dollars a week, and you will be placed at the end of the line. All the girls are on piecework: the faster you are, the higher the pay; a new girl should not hold up the more experienced girls."

"Can I see the assembly line please?" I

31

asked.

"Of course," she said gently, and she got up, put her arm around my shoulders like a friend, and we walked across a hall and up about six steps.

There was an enormous door, so large it was like a church door - when she opened it, it creaked and squeaked very loudly. I was stood on a platform.

Two-hundred eyes looked up at me for just a second, and then they looked down again. It was a sea of blue, every single girl dressed in a uniform.

"You see the end of the line?" June pointed; "This is where you will work. You can start tomorrow, and I will give you time off so that you may arrange your paperwork. I need that social insurance number immediately."

Then she got up and walked to a cupboard. She handed me three blue uniforms. "Try them on in the changing room," she said.

I tried them on, and the smallest one was perfect. I looked into the mirror at my blue uniform, and thought one-hundred dollars a week was fantastic.

With my new job I was able to rent a small apartment. Despite it being small, it was very nice and tidy.

I had been one week in Canada, and I already had a job and a place to live. I felt proud.

It was an interesting experience at first to work in a factory. At first I was worried I would be too slow and would not be able to keep up, but I quickly realised that my fingers could move very fast, and I was convinced that my piano lessons as a child had helped me tremendously. I moved up the assembly line very quickly.

After six months, I was asked to meet again with June.

"I have an opening in the quality control lab. You're good with numbers and you work hard: you will do well," she said, and smiled, got up, and put her arm again around my shoulders.

I got up and hugged her. I was so happy, tears were running down my face.

"Come and see me once in a while, and tell me how you are doing," she said, as she wiped the tears off my face with a Kleenex.

It was in this new job that I met Daniel.

The first time Daniel came into my room he did not say a word, but stood very close to me.

He watched me work.

Since I was concentrating, I could not look back at him. But when I finished I turned to him, and the first thing I noticed was his big, brown eyes. Then I saw his bleached hair - very blond. With his white gloves and white coat he looked immaculate, slim, and actually quite attractive - he reminded me of seeing Damien in his doctor's whites.

I smiled.

He did not smile back.

Daniel was always business-like and professional, although I often caught him staring at me. Not in such a way to make me feel uncomfortable, but that I knew that he liked me a lot. But whilst I thought he was attractive, I did not fancy him. He always asked me the same questions about my work - I felt appreciated.

One day he asked me something different:

"I have a couple of books I would very much like to show you. I could drop them by your place sometime, if you are interested."

"I am interested in everything," I replied.

It was not only through politeness, but also curiosity, that I told him to come to my place the following evening.

## CHAPTER SEVEN

It was exactly seven-thirty when the buzzer in my apartment sounded, followed a few moments later by a gentle knock at my door.

Even though I did not fancy Daniel, I wanted to look smart for him: I had dressed in golden slippers, white trousers, and a white see-through sweater. I had manicured my nails and put matching lipstick on.

I had also tidied up my small apartment so that it looked nice and tidy for him - by removing any clutter it looked slightly bigger.

When I opened the door I saw a very different Daniel to the one dressed in white coats at work.

He wore skin-tight, black trousers and a black turtle-neck sweater. I noticed his white hair, wondering if he dyed it, for it just didn't go with such a young face.

I also saw that he clutched a brown leather suitcase.

The smile on his pale face was strange.

'Something has happened to him,' I thought, 'he looks and acts entirely different from when I saw him in the plant.'

I started to get anxious. Still, I could not turn him away, so I invited him in.

Stepping from the front door into my living room, I beckoned him over to my small sofa.

"Please sit down," I said.

He looked awkward as he did so, a forced casualness in his manner.

He placed the briefcase on his lap and kept both hands on it. I wondered what book could be so important.

Daniel tried so hard to act as if we had been acquainted for a very long time: we exchanged small-talk about the company, the weather, the latest world crisis, and a hint or two about his marital problems.

As we spoke, his hands played nervously with his briefcase.

Strange.

I wondered if it *was* in fact a book, or something else.

I felt nervous.

"What's in the briefcase, Daniel?"

"Books. I told you."

"What books are they?"

"Very special books."

"Show me," I said, unable to hide a tremor in my voice.

He repositioned his briefcase on his lap and opened it with shaky fingers.

Why was he shaking like that? Perhaps I had made a mistake in accepting his invitation.

I began to get scared.

"Let me show you the books," said Daniel, as he reached in.

Oh, how stupid I had been! The way he shook, he would appear to be as scared as I was. But what could he be scared of? I knew he was lying.

My heart was thumping through my chest - I couldn't breathe. I wondered if he had done before whatever he was about to do.

His trembling hand came out and in it was a paperback book.

I was confused.

He handed the paperbacks to me, hiding the front covers with his hands.

I couldn't look at the books yet. Instead, I looked at his dark-brown eyes, to see if I could see any hint of malice.

I saw none - just kindness and fear. And he was scared.

Taking three of the books in my hand, I saw the bizarre, glossy covers for the first time.

I was amazed.

I looked up and caught a glimpse of a man transformed: in that brief moment, the pupils of his eyes had widened noticeably - he looked like he was craving something.

I examined the covers, trying to be as casual as possible, whilst glancing at him from time to time.

I felt relief knowing that whatever this visit was, it was not sinister.

I returned my gaze to the books and studied the cover pictures, the like of which I had never seen: beautiful, tall, slim girls with long black hair, their breasts and erect nipples exposed, dressed in the tiniest leather skirts and the highest leather boots I had ever seen. In their hands were long, leather whips, and at their feet were nude men, on their hands and knees.

I remembered so well that I had told Dan I was interested in "everything" - he had taken my reply quite literally.

I had never seen anything like this - it was a world I was completely ignorant to. The only man I had seen naked was Damien, and I had *never* seen another woman like that.

My heart began to quicken again.

I was excited.

I wanted to know more, but I did not want

Daniel to know that this was new to me.

I tried to hide what were my now-shaking hands. I pretended to look through the books as I tried to recollect my composure. After a few minutes, I was ready.

Laying the books casually aside, I looked straight at Daniel.

His face was wreathed in sweat.

He then did the most bizarre thing: he trembled and began to slide down off of the couch, until he was on the floor on his hands and knees, looking up at me.

Wow.

My stomach tightened and I felt my nipples become erect under the material of my bra.

I had never experienced anything like this before. But I liked the feeling: that this debonair, disciplined businessman had been transformed into a humble creature at my feet.

I didn't know what to do - I just sat there watching Daniel at my feet. He was now staring at the little golden heels of the slipper I was wearing.

After a few moments of silence, he spoke: "Will you be my mistress? I haven't had a mistress for a long time! I had one once, but I was not obedient enough to be a good slave - I was obstinate and refractory."

I could hardly believe my ears: *Mistress? Slave?* What was he talking about! "Slave" is only a word I had heard in school, in history class, and it is something grotesque. What was this new meaning of the word, where a successful businessman speaks of being the slave of a woman? And *mistress?* What is this!?

Sparring for time, and to avoid saying the wrong thing, I replied as calmly as I could: "Who was your last mistress?"

Without lifting his head, he replied: "She was a Russian woman - her name was Nina…"

Daniel stayed on the floor. He was clearly waiting for some kind of instruction.

I could not understand this. I wondered if he really would do as I asked. All I wanted in that moment was to learn more.

"I need you to do something for me - to arrange something," I said, trying to remain calm.

"Certainly, Mistress - it is my pleasure to do this, since you demand it."

The word "mistress" again - it excited me and it gave me the confidence to say what I wanted:

"I would like to meet Nina."

## CHAPTER EIGHT

A week later Daniel called on me: "Nina is hosting a party at her mansion tonight."

We drove there without speaking.

I'm sure Daniel wondered what I was going to do. What Dan did not know, as we drove across Toronto, was that *I* didn't know what I was going to do, either.

We turned off into a large country estate.

On either side there were ponds, each centred with a splashing fountain; coloured floodlights played through the flowering shrubs and gave the whole place the look of a fairyland.

I was so excited.

We parked at the front of the house and Daniel helped me out of the car and up the broad, stone steps to the front door.

He knocked.

We waited.

I rubbed my arms, as I felt cold. Daniel took his jacket off and placed it on my shoulders. As he did, the front door was opened by a lady in her forties - she was slim and tall, and wore a green satin, ankle-length gown.

At first I thought it was Nina, and I felt a little bit disappointed. She wasn't unattractive, but she was older than I thought - in her late forties - and wore too much make-up. I had imagined Nina as some stunning creature.

Then Daniel introduced her as: "Lisa, a friend of Nina."

Before Lisa greeted me, we heard the screech of tires rounding the gravel of the drive. We all turned around to see a white convertible car drive up to the front of the steps.

Driving it was a single lady.

"Nina!" exclaimed Lisa.

When she stepped out of the car, she took my breath away.

She was the most stunning woman I had ever seen. She had long, blonde hair, was tall and slim, with a tiny waist and large breasts. She wore skin-tight leather trousers and a bright red sweater that clung to her every curve.

I turned to Daniel and his mouth was hanging open. I could see why he was so wounded at losing this Nina - I would have done anything for her.

Following Nina out of the car was a huge boxer dog.

I felt myself getting more and more nervous as she approached.

After Lisa had greeted her, she said: "Nina, this is Angelique - a friend Dan brought along."

Nina stared at me, like she was studying some exotic animal.

"You must be Swedish or Norwegian," she said; "I can tell by your height and your lovely, fine, blonde hair."

Nina continued, without waiting for an answer from me: "I am Russian, but I have been in Canada for a very long time. Have you come over recently?"

I nodded.

"Well, I must tell you," she continued: "a party in Canada is different from one in Europe." She put her arm around my shoulders, as if we had been friends a long time. She smiled, looked at me, and walked with me, up the steps, into the house.

"Here, as you will soon see, all the women sit at one side of the room, huddled together, talking about the big things in their lives, while the men stand on the other side like a bunch of starved bulls, boasting to each other about their last 'killing' on the market."

Nina gave me a tour of the house. Every man we passed smiled at Nina, then looked in surprise at me, whilst trying to keep the corner of their eyes on the wife. Each of the women in the house looked down as Nina passed, and looked up with half a sneer at me.

"Let's get away from these crackling hens and find somewhere quiet, where we can get acquainted."

She called a waiter, who came rushing over; "Two double vodkas on-the-rocks – we'll be on the terrace upstairs."

As we went down the broad hall to the stairs, we found Daniel - I had completely forgotten about him. He was sat on a stool, nursing a whisky and soda.

"Daniel, you have been a good slave to bring this beautiful little animal to me," said Nina. "Now I will look after her. You run along into the hen-house downstairs and see what you can promote. I'll see that Angelique gets home safely!"

With that, Daniel left, and we continued the tour.

At the top of the heavily carpeted stairs, Nina pushed open the door of the master bedroom and walked through to the terrace.

She stood at the railings, smiled at me and motioned for me to sit down on a white sofa that had a view of the entire gardens.

It was an amazing sight.

When the barman brought our drinks, Nina sat down beside me.

She was so close I thought I could hear her heart beat. Or maybe it was mine; I was so nervous.

"Tell me about yourself, Angelique."

"I don't think there is much to know."

"Nonsense. A beautiful creature like you doesn't suddenly drop from the sky in my lap - and I would love you in my lap. So, tell me this story."

So, I began to speak to her. I told her about my home in France, Damien, Paris, the men in the bar and Daniel.

Now, I would not normally speak so frankly to a stranger, but Nina had made me feel so at ease. She listened to me for twenty minutes and did not say a word – no-one had listened to me like that before.

When I had finished, she stood up and went into the bedroom.

She came out seconds later holding a white leather riding crop.

Goose pimples arose all over my skin and I let out a shiver.

Nina flicked the leather crop through the air, like she was hitting a creature with it that wasn't there.

"I see that you have always reacted submissively towards men throughout your life. Why is this?"

"I thought I was supposed to," I answered,

"Women are taught that life consists of pleasing a man, caring for the home, and that real love consists of giving. But you found that men are usually taking and not giving, Didn't you?"

"Yes," I replied.

"I always wanted to find a man who would be a god," she said: "somebody to look up to, somebody to lean upon, somebody who would lead me... but I never found such a man - I found only imagined power and crass egotism: *that's* what the male is made of. Often, I have thought of the great women who actually ruled men, like Isabella of Spain, who ruled half of Europe and all of the known New World, or Elizabeth the First, of England, whose ships controlled the commerce of the entire world... Catherine the Great, of Russia, who reigned over a subcontinent. All of these queens had slaves, through whom they ruled, governed, and controlled nations and empires."

She threw her head back and gulped her glass of vodka in one mouthful. Then she laughed into the air, spreading her arms.

"I am not a queen," she said, "but I do have slaves - many of them; intelligent slaves and ignorant slaves."

I gawked.

Nina simply laughed as the barman returned with more drinks, which Nina seized without a word, then waved him away.

As he closed the door softly, she handed me a drink and took up a position with her back to the railing. Looking down at me, she spoke slowly:

"Angelique, you are such an exquisite, lovely creature," she said, "You are almost too beautiful to be loved by a mere man. You were born to be the *ruler* of men - the *master* of men! Those big, limpid pools of turquoise will melt the gaze of the toughest man who walks the face of the earth.

"Your body is the body of a perfect female: tiny bones that are invisible - notwithstanding the fact that you haven't an ounce of surplus fat anywhere; luscious curves of breasts; hips and legs that beckon the caress of any man with an ounce of blood in his veins. And, what I sometimes think are most important of all: your extremities - your nose, ears, hands and feet are superbly feminine."

Blood rushed into my face. Nobody had ever described me like that. I had never seen myself like that. Damien had once or twice said that I was pretty.

"Some of these men kneeling at your feet will call you simply 'Mistress'. Some will call you 'Princess', some will call you 'Queen'. And then, my gorgeous, dazzling female, I urge you to take them - subjugate them slowly but completely, and flog them mercilessly, until all the horrible products of the male ego have been destroyed.

"What happened to you with Damien will never happen again!"

## CHAPTER NINE

"There is one more man I want to introduce you to, now that we have become acquainted," said Nina, leading me back downstairs to the party.

"Geoffrey is a man who has been around - he has been to several of the financially well-organized private clubs in New York, where they host everything from orgies to bondage and flagellate sessions, and, what's more, he's English. You know the English: they have been doing these things there for many years."

As we entered the living room, I saw Geoffrey.

He looked more like an Arab than an Englishman: he was very tall, with pitch-black hair and dark brown eyes. He wore a well-fitted white suit, but without a shirt! His bare torso was toned, with dark skin. He was one of the most attractive men I have seen.

'Girls must follow him everywhere,' I thought.

"Geoffrey, this is Angelique. You and she

ought to get together some time."

Geoffrey looked at me, bent down and kissed my hand.

He leaned against a wall, took out a golden cigarette case, and lit a cigarette. Nina then took one herself.

He looked at Nina and smiled. "The next time I see you, Nina," he said, "it will probably be to invite you to have dinner with me, for old times' sake, before I finally go away for the holiday that I have been waiting to go on for six years. It seems that my business is finally close to settlement, in a way that will enable me to make a fresh start."

"Oh yes, how many times have you made a fresh start?" said Nina. Taking her thumb, she slowly touched him from the base of his neck down to his belt, and I saw a red line she made with her nail appear right on his bare chest. As she did this, he continued to speak:

"Oh, this *is* a fresh start, but first I plan to go away and reward myself with a holiday. I will fly over the pole from Edmonton to Amsterdam, then to Hamburg, Germany, to see the Alster - the lake in the middle of town..."

I could not believe it - she has the audacity to scratch him so hard that there is a red line on his chest. What is this man feeling? Why is he not reacting?

Nina blew smoke into his eyes and moved closer still. She took her thumb again and made a second line with her nail. She must have pressed harder, because it was more visible from his neck down to his belt, and actually bleeding.

He grabbed her hand when she was down at his belt, but continued talking:

"...at the most, I want to get a panoramic view of the world's history, without becoming confused by detailed sightseeing."

"Well, well, well," said Nina. "God, can you ramble on?! I wonder if I can remember all the cities you've just mentioned. How impressive. That leaves just enough time for you to meet Angelique."

He smiled, glanced at me, and said: "I would not miss it for the world."

With that, he kissed my hand again, smiled at Nina, and walked away.

"He must be super-rich," I said. "He is fabulous-looking and seems to be very educated. He knows all about historical attractions, literally across the world - he must be a catch for any girl."

"Yes, but he has feet of clay, which is to say he has a weakness or hidden flaw: even though he is a greatly-admired and respected person, and yes, he is well off, and yes, he is educated, you will be very surprised when you *really* meet him, and analyse his character - I wonder if you will still think the way you think today."

Nina walked over and closed the door. Then she stopped, shot her head round and stared at me.

I felt cold.

"What, Nina?"

She looked me slowly up and down and stepped towards me without answering.

I shivered.

Nina stepped closer, playing with her nail - the same nail she had scratched Geoffrey with. Her hands were so beautiful. I realised I was holding my breath and let out a huge sigh.

I shivered again.

"My home is an arena for adult fantasies where the mind is free and inhibitions are gone."

I hadn't felt like this since Michael had described kissing between my legs.

"Everybody needs escapes Angelique - don't you agree?"

I opened my mouth to speak but no words came out.

Nina stepped closer.

Her face came close to mine.

Her mouth was open like mine.

I thought she was going to kiss me. I left my mouth open.

Then Nina pursed her lips and blew a cloud of smoke into my mouth.

Nina smiled. "Some people find it quite sexy for a woman to be smoking."

I felt my eyes water. I squeezed them shut and looked down. I felt so silly. What was I doing?

Nina lifted my chin with her hand.

"Geoffrey loves to play. So, all we do is play - remember that. I would like you to help me with my next session with Geoffrey. You will invite him to your apartment and do exactly as I say."

My face erupted into a smile. I was glad that I would see Nina again.

Nina continued to hold my face, before leaning forward. This time I closed my eyes. I felt a light kiss on my cheek.

I let out a sigh as all the tension in my body went. I opened my eyes, smiling again.

"I think we can be very close friends," said Nina.

I knew there was nothing I would want more.

## CHAPTER TEN

Previously, I had only skimmed through the pages of the books Dan had left, but since agreeing to help Nina, I knew I had to learn fast. I re-read all of the books. Their pages catapulted me into this new world. At the same time, I was in contact with Nina, who was giving me clear instructions as to what to do and how it all worked.

A week later, Geoffrey telephoned me. Nina had written down on paper the exact words I should say to him:

"Yes, Geoffrey, I will see you two weeks from tonight. You will come at exactly 7:00pm - not earlier, not later. You will ask no questions and go with me to a place I have prepared."

There was a long silence.

I was worried I had messed it up.

Then he said, almost meekly: "Yes, Princess," and hung up.

I reported to Nina right away.

Nina said I had done very well. I felt so

proud.

"Nina, wouldn't it be better for me to meet him at yours? My apartment is not big enough for two people."

"Nonsense, Angelique. You see how eager he is to meet up with you? He has even had to cancel his holiday to see you. Oh, what a surprise I will bestow upon him. He won't be noticing anything apart from you. I have told Geoffrey that he is not to ask you any questions and he is not to lay a finger on you. Oh, and don't forget to tell him to sit on the floor when he arrives at your place."

I wasn't sure I could ask such a thing as it seemed rude, but since Nina had insisted, so I agreed.

Geoffrey rang my buzzer at exactly seven p.m..

The very preciseness of his punctuality gave my confidence a much needed boost: I felt that since he had obeyed me in a small thing, he would obey me in other things too.

When I answered the door, Geoffrey was standing there in a well-fitted gray suit and white shirt, which clung to his toned physique.

He was carrying a large leather shoulder bag.

I invited him in and he immediately started

to question me as to my interests.

"No questions, Geoffrey - Nina said. So please don't ask me anything as I won't be able to answer you."

"Fine," he said and went to sit on the sofa.

Trying to maintain control, I quickly said: "You may sit on the floor," just as Nina had instructed me.

He looked at me, sighed, then sat on the floor.

I felt better.

"I brought some things with me I thought you might like."

I thought: 'You are the second person to come to my apartment and the second person to bring me a gift. I wonder what strange thing it will be this time, and where it will lead me.' I could not say this aloud, so I simply said: "You may give them to me."

He reached into a purple bag and produced a bottle of Champagne.

My face erupted into a large smile. 'How sweet,' I thought, but then I remembered to try and stay calm, and said: "There are glasses on the table - you may open it, pour me one and have one yourself."

Geoffrey picked up the bottle of Champagne and squeezed the top off - I squeezed my eyes shut as it popped. Then I watched him pour it into the glasses. He was so handsome and so stylish.

"What would you like to toast to, Geoffrey?" I asked.

"To everything!" he replied.

'How strange,' I thought.

Then he reached back to the bag.

"I have something else for you, which you might like, but I will have to demonstrate it on you."

This worried me a little, but I decided to go ahead; "Okay, but whatever you do, you are not allowed to touch me, please."

Geoffrey scoffed, and then he agreed.

"You must lay on the floor, Princess," he said. "I promise you I will not hurt you."

"You are not even to touch me."

"No part of me shall touch you."

I carefully lay on the floor so as not to disturb my clothes.

Geoffrey then unwrapped a black, leather-covered box about twelve inches high and twenty inches wide. One of the long sides was open, and the other side had a semicircle opening.

He placed it very gently over my head, being careful not to touch me with his hands. The semicircle opening went over my neck and the other open side allowed my hair to fall onto the floor.

Looking straight up I saw that inside the roof of the box was a mirror, fixed at such an angle that I had a horizontal view along my body.

It was a mesmerising sight.

I could see my breasts standing up right in front, inches from my eyes. I could even see the outline of my nipples grow as I admired how sexy my body looked.

I had never seen or felt this way about myself before.

As I was enjoying this feeling, I saw Geoffrey reach over, and with one hand, press down on the box, which pressed against my neck in such a way that I felt helpless.

With the other hand, he motioned near my breasts.

I felt caught.

Then I felt his hand grabbing me, cupping me and feeling my nipple through the fabric of my clothes.

It felt my neck was in a vice so I couldn't move my head. And all I could see was his hand on my breast.

My body felt ice cold. It was horrible.

I struggled up against the box.

Geoffrey released his hand from the box.

As I got up and lifted the box aside, I saw a mischievous smile on his face.

I felt shocked. At that particular moment I hated him. He had entrapped me. He had induced a state of panic in me – yes, just for a second, but he had managed it.

I comforted myself that when Nina was done with him that smile will be gone.

I got up, composed myself quickly and said nonchalantly: "I find it interesting - you may leave it with me. But now we must go, as it is getting late - we have to see Nina."

## CHAPTER ELEVEN

Even on the drive to Nina's house, Geoffrey could not do what he was told. Despite me repeating my no question rule, which was designed by Nina to protect me from my inexperience, he continued to badger me. I felt relieved when we arrived at her abode on the other side of the city.

The house looked different to the last time I was here, as it was now in total darkness. The moonlight allowed me to see up to the front door. Nina had told me that it would be unlocked.

Inside, I told Geoffrey to wait in the hallway, whilst I made my way through to the living room, which was visible only by candle light.

When I reached the room I saw Nina with her back to me, sat in a rocking chair, which she moved slowly to and fro.

'This is surreal,' I thought.

Nina had her face obscured by a huge black hat, and at the back her long, blonde hair fell over her shoulders. Her hands and arms were encased in long, black kid-gloves, her feet and legs in shiny, long, black leather boots.

A huge black veil, loosely draped over her body, showed each of her breasts.

In one gloved hand, she held a long whip, which she slowly tapped against her boot. In the other hand, she held a chain tethering the same muscular boxer dog.

Nina looked so different. I stood transfixed.

The sound of a man's footsteps coming down the hallway stirred Nina to rise, turning her head, and I found myself looking into her beautiful blue eyes.

She laughed softly, her eyes full of joy as she saw my puzzlement. She whispered to me: "I see your bewilderment - this is a fantasy world that you have entered, and *I* create the dreams. Now, did Geoffrey behave himself at yours?"

I nodded.

"Really? That does not sound like him at all. Did he ask you any questions… did he touch you?"

I nodded.

"Okay. I have laid some clothes in my bedroom - I want you to go and change. I will teach this fellow not to walk around in my house."

61

Despite her instruction to change, I remained where I was and watched Nina stalk silently up to Geoffrey. When Nina was directly behind him, he turned around.

Then Nina slapped him hard across the face with her gloved hands - several times on each cheek.

The sound of the leather against the skin on his face made me shudder.

"Get down on your knees without delay, slave!"

His body folded as he moved to obey this command. I watched this powerful female, who, with just a sentence, had humbled this great bulk of a man.

"Go ahead and kiss my boots!" She repeated: "Kiss them!"

He lowered his back until his head almost touched the floor, and he obeyed, kissing her boots.

Nina raised her hand.

*Whack!*

Nina brought the whip she held in her other hand down, and slashed it across Geoffrey's back.

His only movement was to withdraw his lips slightly from the boots.

"I didn't tell you to stop. Kiss them, slave,"

she hissed.

He started again to smother her boots with kisses.

Then she raised her hand, and again brought the whip down onto his back.

*Whack!*

Again, I shuddered.

*Whack.*

*Whack.*

The sound of each whack caused me to shudder. But I was enjoying the feeling. I was getting excited.

Illuminated in light from the moon, the whip seemed to dance in the air, before each blow struck Geoffrey's back. It was an image that I would not forget.

Remembering Nina's instructions to change, I ran to her bedroom and undressed until I was nude.

On her bed, Nina had laid out a flimsy tunic, which I put over my head - it was so short I could feel a cold draught on my bum. I caught a sight of myself in one of Nina's four huge mirrors: I looked like a Roman slave girl.

"Angelique, come on down. I want you," shouted Nina.

Because of the light in the bedroom, when I re-entered the living room, I could see nothing.

*Whack!*

I felt a burning crack on my back, that seared my skin under the flimsy tunic.

I dropped to my knees and found myself looking at Nina's boots in the flickering candlelight.

'God, what is happening?' I thought.

Then I felt a something cold and heavy on my shoulders. It was a chain.

"Chain him," said Nina.

I struggled to untangle the weight from my body, and a second blow hit me.

*Whack.*

'Oh, God, what is this?' I felt like crying. I was so scared. 'She must really hate me,' I thought, as I tried feverishly to untangle myself.

Nina laughed; "You need more training!"

Then, with a single movement, she unwound the chain from my body. She stepped over me.

"Kneel there, where you can see my boots, but don't touch them – they've been licked by a dirty male slave. Once he is chained, dance right in front of him."

Nina wound the chain around Geoffrey, fastening his wrists and ankles together with a lock. He looked like a huge ball, in an almost kneeling position, with his head down, rocking

64

back and forth.

"Dance," said Nina.

"What?"

*Whack.*

This time, the whip wrapped around my body and tore at my breasts. I jumped like an animal trying to defend myself.

Nina was too quick. She seized me with one hand pinning my wrists behind my back, and with the other, she grabbed my hair, and very slowly pulled my face up close to hers. I felt her warm, silky body against mine, and this soothed me.

At that moment I just wanted Nina.

All I could think was: 'Do not leave me alone - stay with me.' I had been alone, without a family or anybody close to me, for so long.

She relaxed her grip to a gentle touch. Then she kissed me softly; "Come, my little animal, don't fight against me - you will only lose."

I threw my arms around her.

I felt the warmth of her body against mine; I felt her strength as she continued to hold me.

"Now, when I whip Geoffrey, I want you to dance."

I looked into her eyes and just nodded.

Nina let go of me and I dropped to the floor. Then she then turned her attention to Geoffrey.

She whipped him.

*Whack.*

I got up off the floor and danced.

Nervously at first - I kept pulling my tunic down over my bum, and didn't want to move too much in case Geoffrey or Nina could see me.

But as I began to dance, I felt more confident. The situation was surreal enough anyway, so dancing seemed almost natural.

I continued to dance as Geoffrey was whipped.

I admired the way Nina handled the whip: like a ballerina handles a ribbon.

At times the impact from the whip caused Geoffrey to almost hit his face on the floor.

Nina stopped for a moment and undid Geoffrey's belt and pulled his trousers down. Then, she opened up his shirt and rolled it up.

I could see his back and his buttocks, they were bright red.

Nina took a riding crop.

"Amsterdam," she hissed, and then she hit him. Hard.

"Hamburg," she hissed, and hit him again.

"Munich" - she hit him again; each time he cried in pain. "Prague: one stroke... Moscow (my city), slave: two hits... Athens: one... Istanbul: one... Rome, to see the Pope!" she shrieked:

"Two... and, finally Gibraltar. I hope you have a great time on you holiday!" screamed Nina.

Then she paused to remove the long wig she had on. She blew the hair that fell into her face away. Then she winked at me.

"And this is for Angelique."

*Whack.*

"This is for touching her."

*Whack.*

"This is for boring her with your stupid questions."

*Whack.*

"And this is for not doing what you are told slave!"

*Whack. Whack. Whack.*

I continued to dance.

Nina continued to hit him.

I could see the welts on Geoffrey's back, increasing in size and brightness. Despite this, Geoffrey did not complain.

Nina hit him a final time, before dropping the riding crop to the floor.

We rose together to leave the room, but just before we left, Nina tossed a key at him.

"You there, preposterous slave: I have better things to do than waste any more time with you. Unchain yourself and leave the house very quietly. I don't want to see or hear you again.

Since I don't want you again, I will ask
Angelique if she wants you. If so, she shall
summon you."

Then she put her arm round me and said:
"Let us go, my darling, where we will be more
comfortable and where we won't smell the sweat
of that stupid slave."

## CHAPTER TWELVE

"How do you know he is not mad? And how do you know that he will not turn and beat you up one of these days?" I asked.

We were sitting on the sofa outside, on the terrace overlooking the garden.

"Oh, my darling," she laughed, "this is what he wanted. This is exactly why he is here. He got what he asked for and more - much more. He is indeed very satisfied!"

"But things could go wrong, couldn't they? How do you protect yourself then, to prevent any mistakes? And how do you know what they will accept?"

"It would be a cliché to tell you that it will come with experience. There is practice, instruction, skill, training, observation, experimental knowledge and a lot of feeling. But most important of all, you have to listen – don't talk, just listen."

"Why did you tell Geoffrey that he will see me?" I asked.

"Oh, you don't have to see him," she answered with a smile, "but I think that he is definitely your type! Just watching you stare at him, I knew. And besides, I am tired of him. I will give him to you as a special present: your first, own slave. Perhaps also your first lover? Perhaps as your first real companion? It's your selection."

"Geoffrey may not want to see me at all."

Nina laughed; "He cancelled his world trip to see you. Don't be so naïve."

We sat very close to each other, and she put her arm around me, and stroked my arm and back - goose-pimples popped up on my skin where she touched me.

"Angelique, we are females, and being a complete female, love, is something ever present in our bodies, minds and souls. We all want love, don't we? But you have been the victim of a succession of selfish, egotistical, self-centred men, who had no respect for your soul, mind or body."

"This is not true, Nina. My Dad loved me and so did Damien."

"Excuse me? We were sitting exactly here when you told me Damien was extremely selfish and self-centred. Your father had no respect for the soul and mind of his daughter. What did they accomplish with their actions?

"There will always be fear that lurks very near the surface, in your dealings with every man you meet. I can tell you right now that fear will consume you, even though it may be frequently intermingled with love for a man."

"I don't understand. Why are you saying this?"

"You ran away, right? Fear has in turn spawned your passion for freedom, and I can tell you right now that these elements - fear and caution - will constantly replace your love urge, until you achieve your goal."

"And what is my goal?"

"Your goal might be described as becoming permanently convinced that you have found a man who respects your soul, your mind, and your body, and with whom you can share that perfect freedom that comes only with total surrender."

"Total surrender?" I asked.

"When you reciprocally share this mystery, you will have that perfect mutual love, and you will have freedom."

It was two in the morning when we left Nina's home.

When she stepped out of her house, she locked the front door and lifted up the doormat. There was an envelope, and she stuffed it into her pocket.

"Don't you want to check the living room for Geoffrey?" I said before we left.

"No need," she said; "he is long gone."

"How do you know?" I asked anxiously.

"My husband is home," she said, "and my dog. Do you think that they would let him move anywhere but out the door?"

Stepping through the front door of my apartment, I felt a return to reality. I wondered whether this had just been a dream. It seemed unreal.

I went to the kitchen to look for the glasses me and Geoffrey had drunk Champagne from. They weren't on the side waiting to be washed, as I had expected, but instead were neatly put away as if they had never been used.

I went back into the lounge and stopped.

A shiver shot through me.

Next to the sofa was the mirrored box that Geoffrey had given me.

It had been real.

# THE MIRRORED BOX

## CHAPTER THIRTEEN

It was Sunday.

I was exhausted.

I made myself a coffee and hung up the clothes I had worn at the party with Nina. Then I opened up my purse. It was stuffed with money. I counted it: one-thousand dollars in hundred and fifty dollar bills. I called Nina.

"There is a lot of money in my purse. Is it possible that you could explain it to me?" I said.

"Is your time not precious?" she asked. "Have you not spent hours planning and executing the party? Nothing in this life is for free, my darling. You have earned it, and you most certainly deserve it. Besides, it is just a token of my appreciation, and it was Geoffrey's gift, meant for the both of us."

"But Nina," I replied, "this is one month of my wages. It is just so much – I'm totally shocked."

"I'm glad you're shocked," she said, "and I am sure it will come in handy. I know you may have a lot of questions right now and you are anxious to get answers, so let me explain something: I don't think about money, and I don't discuss it. People who think about money all the time don't know anything about living. For me, money arrives just as the rain arrives when the ground needs it. It is usually more than I expect, and at times I am also utterly surprised. Don't ever think or speak about money any more, never ever - I despise the subject. Think that you are very rich. Remember the room in Paris where you had washed yourself with a hose in a basement? That won't happen again." With that, she hung up.

As soon as I put the phone down it rang again - it startled me. I picked it up, expecting it to be Nina again, but this time it was Geoffrey, and my heart started to beat faster.

"How are you, Angelique? Did you have any visions in your sleep? Do you like to daydream of me travelling around the world for fourteen days?"

"I remember all the cities you wanted to visit," I said.

"So did Nina," he answered; "Nina and her photographic mind. I remembered the hits with the whip: one for each city, with two for Moscow and two for Rome. But she forgot one city: Cairo, and the mysteries of the pyramids."

"Yes, I guess she forgot Cairo," I said.

"Come with me, Angelique. That you exist transforms the world for me. I think of you and I am happy. I can think of the constant change of expression on your face and I am enchanted. I see your lips in my mind's eye. The combination of sensuousness and imperiousness delights me."

Wow. I was shocked. Damien had never said anything like that to me before.

"Listen, Angelique. Whenever I am in a beautiful place, or listen to beautiful music, I will have you by my side, and the beauty will be double. I think of your honesty of mind and am impelled to greater honesty myself. If this were all, would it not be enough? You don't have to spend a penny - it will all be paid for. See the world with me, Angelique."

His words caught me off-guard and astonished me. For a second, I imagined what it would be like travelling first class around the world for fourteen days, and how much I would love to see all the places he had described. 'My God, how he describes travelling with me,' I thought, 'how romantic.'

And the way he speaks and the words he uses - I feel I could melt.

Because I was silent and said nothing, he continued: "But, in fact, there is more. I think you have a capacity for originality, and once you have found all the time you need to develop your originality and you also find time to spend with me, I will be truly blessed, for when I am with you, my heart is at peace. I am saying all this, and I do not wish to tie you or to confine you. I wish you to be free, and if then, being free, you choose to rest in my arms, or in some other way to draw sustenance from me - wholly by choice and wholly from the movement of your Spirit - then I will be truly honoured."

'He wants me to develop,' I thought. 'He puts me on a pedestal - almost looks up to me. He wants me to be free. He is the opposite of Damien, and I never knew a man could talk like that.'

"Thank you, Geoffrey," I said. "Have a great trip."

I hung up. I had to call Nina.

"Geoffrey wants to take me around the world - imagine that!"

There was a long pause before Nina spoke. "He is your slave now, and you must think very clearly about what you want to do with him. If he is your slave, you can never ever have a social relationship with him - this is totally out of the question," she said sternly. "You have to make a choice: either your lover and companion, or your slave, but never, ever both."

"He wants me to develop, and he puts me on a pedestal! How great is that? Do you know if he is married?"

Nina uttered: "He is not - I know this for sure. He had several wives, and he has several children. I have yet to meet the female not struck by his looks and his fancy cars, and he can wrap a woman right around his little finger. He can talk up a storm, and he is very intelligent and educated.

"And I will say it again: he is your *slave*. You cannot sleep with a slave. If you want a relationship with him you must give him up as a slave, but then you will lose your power and you will be like every other woman that he encounters. He won't put you on a pedestal then, I can assure you! If you want to keep on seeing him and to be in control, then he must be your slave. He is a slave - remember that, my darling. Now I have to go. And you have to think."

For the second time that day Nina hung up on me.

## CHAPTER FOURTEEN

I had been working as usual and trying to get on with my life, but Nina and Geoffrey would not leave my thoughts. Five weekends went by before she called me again.

"Nina!" I realised my voice sounded the same as Lisa's did, the first night I had met her at the party, when she had called out Nina's name.

"Are you alone right now?" she asked.

"Yes."

"If you remove the cloth from any part of a man's body, which part of a man's body would you see first?"

"I don't know, Nina - I don't understand the question."

"What do you think you look sexiest in?"

"I have no idea. Why are you asking me something like that?"

"Well … well... well…" she sighed. There was an audibly long, deep breath. "I have decided that you will handle three slaves next time you are in my place."

"You must be kidding! What kind of slaves, Nina?"

"Never mind - I hate to talk on the phone. But I know you can handle three."

"Explain to me what you are talking about - I am confused. Tell me about the slaves please, Nina. Are you joking?"

"You are gorgeous, Angelique – magnificent… ravishing! Oh, you are so difficult to talk to. Geez, you will hold your submissive clients' power in your hands. You are just role-playing, so be creative! Be at mine at five-thirty."

"But, work!"

"Just be there."

"Okay, Nina. I will be there."

Even in the fading light I could clearly see the vast array of different coloured flowers in Nina's garden. I expected fairies to come out of the trees – it was that pretty.

When Nina opened the door I stood and gawped.

Nina looked like the women on the covers of the books I had read.

She wore black fishnet stockings under a tiny red skirt, and black leather stiletto boots with red soles. She also had on a red corset, which squeezed her tiny waist in and pushed her breasts out. A black veil she wore on her head framed her figure perfectly.

For the second time, I knew why men fell at her feet.

"I hope it is clear that this is all about you, and your pleasure and amusement," she said. And, without any further explanation, she escorted me into her bedroom to dress.

I was filled with excitement when I saw what was laid out on the bed: black elbow-length leather gloves, black stockings, black leather stiletto shoes and a black satin strapless corselet.

Nina watched me as I undressed.

I removed my street clothes, but kept my knickers on.

"Come on, Angelique," Nina said: "take off your knickers - you will wear this corselet nude."

I turned my back to her and took off my knickers.

I had never been nude in front of anyone before, except Damien and my Mum.

Nina came up behind me.

"Lift your arms up."

I lifted them. I could feel her breath on the back of my neck and shoulders. It made my body tingle and my nipples erect.

'Oh, God - I hope she doesn't notice how aroused I am,' I thought.

Nina took the corselet and wrapped it around my body. Then she closed the zip and tied up the strings - so tight I could hardly breathe.

"Spread your legs."

I shifted my legs apart.

I could feel the cool air of the bedroom on my pussy.

Then I felt the leather of her gloves on my legs as she pulled on my stockings.

Finally, she took my feet and squeezed them into the boots.

When I looked in the mirror, I was amazed.

I looked like Nina. I never thought I could look anything like this.

But, still I felt embarrassed.

"Nina, I can't wear this."

"Why not? You look beautiful."

"But, Nina, I am not *you*. This is ridiculous. You can see my breasts, and you had me take off my knickers - now anyone can see my pussy."

"I hope they do : you look beautiful. Too beautiful for any man, or any of the beasts I have prepared for you tonight."

I shuddered.

"Come on," she said.

Nina led me down the stairs into her basement. It was the first time I had been here, and it was pitch-black - I had to hold the hand-rail on either side to guide myself down.

When we reached the bottom, I opened a door into a spectacular mirrored room, which stretched on into infinity.

Each wall was covered from top to bottom with mirrors. Glow-sticks emitted bright light in all different colours, reflected into sparkles and stars. My sight was overwhelmed by this amazing light-show.

As I walked through the room I saw my reflection. Until now I had never liked looking into the mirror - Damien had said my arms and legs were too thin, and my neck was too long. Nobody had ever said my body was amazing, and every time I had seen a reflection of myself I had hated the image.

But now I saw myself, I looked like Nina, and more beautiful than I ever had thought at any other point in my life.

Nina saw me looking at my reflection and stopped. She placed her hand on my shoulder and said: "Never forget how awesome you actually are - you are an exceptionally gorgeous woman."

Then she kissed me on my neck.

I felt my body shudder.

We continued through the basement, into the next room, which looked like a dungeon. At the very back was a door leading to Nina's garden, which was covered by a black velvet curtain.

Above were rows of hooks dangling from the ceiling.

Fixed to one of them was an old man - he appeared to be a hundred years old. I thought Nina was a maniac and started to feel sorry for him. I reminded myself that the men had to agree to this, but still I could not understand. Perhaps Nina had a reason for treating him like this. I wanted to ask him normally, but remembered this role-play, and Nina was watching, so I said: "Old slave, what have you done? What are you here for? What have you done to bring this punishment upon yourself?"

"Oh, beautiful angel woman," he replied with pleading in his voice; "whip me! I beat up a very young girl. Oh, angel woman, whip me without mercy!"

I felt sick when he told me this. He reminded me of all the men who groped me when I was a waitress in Paris. 'Man-beast,' I thought, 'beating up a young girl – you'll get it.'

Nina looked at me and placed a small leather whip in my hand. Then she came behind me, like a mother might do to a child, and held my arms. She guided my arm back and threw it forward, causing the whip to snap down on the man's back.

The sound of the whip, and the feeling of it connecting rippled through my body… I felt like my pussy had been kissed for the first time.

"More, more, more!" cried the man, swinging in the chains.

Before I could swing, Nina stopped me and unchained the man, even as he continued to shout:

"More. Whip me more! More!"

Nina grabbed him by the head and dragged him out of the room.

I was amazed.

I was alone and unnerved - no slave, no whip, no Nina.

I looked around the rest of the room - all of the other walls were covered with curtains.

Then I saw a slight movement behind one of them, and I remembered that Nina had said there were three slaves.

I didn't know whether to wait for Nina, and whether she would be angry if I didn't. So, I decided just to peek, just to see.

I crept over towards the curtain.

The heels on my stilettos clicked the floor as I did.

I pulled the curtain aside and saw a man in his early twenties, holding a bouquet of red carnations in his outstretched hand.

I was bewildered. 'What is happening?' I thought. 'This cannot be real.'

I looked at the man - he looked scared.

I was sure that he had never in his life been in a place like this. So young and so handsome, he looked like he should be at a prom, not a place like this.

He looked at me, but did not speak.

I took the arrangement of flowers from him, and as I did so, a small leather lash fell to the floor.

Yet again, I thought that this whole thing was bizarre. I couldn't comprehend this happening.

Then I thought that this was some kind of test by Nina. Perhaps she wanted to see if I would have the strength to lash someone on my own.

I thought: 'I will meet her test and deal with this man, or slave.' – If he was that.

"Do you want me to lash you?"

The man nodded.

"Then hand it to me."

Without speaking, he reached down quickly, picked up the lash with trembling fingers, and handed it to me.

"What's your name?" I said, formally.

He whispered the word: "Percy."

I couldn't lash him with his clothes on, so he would need to undress. But how can I tell a man to undress? I wanted to try it, to test out this power.

"Strip," I said.

He just looked at me, not moving.

I felt a little bit angry, like he was mocking me, or perhaps he just did not hear me.

"I told you to strip. Do it immediately," I said.

I watched him undress.

I watched him take of his jacket, and then he took off his shoes, then his socks. I couldn't believe that he would undress any more.

Then he took off his shirt and I saw his slim body, with just a trace of muscle around his chest and stomach. He took off his trousers and I saw his long, toned legs. Then he took off his boxer shorts.

Only the second time I had seen a naked man in front of me like this, and yet it felt like it was the first.

He was so good-looking I normally would have felt intimidated. But I knew I had made him undress, and that he was, at least for now, my slave. I knew that I had the power, and that gave me the confidence to be with this beautiful, naked man, confidence that I would never have had if I had been with him in any other situation.

I was unsure what to do next.

I saw a chain and a lock on the floor.

So I decided to chain him.

I touched his body as much as I could whilst I chained his arms and legs.

I didn't know what to do next.

The lash.

I took it, but didn't want to hit him with it. So, instead, I ran the tassels all over his skin, giving me a chance to look at every inch of his body.

In truth, this was the first time I had seen a man's body in this much detail. With Damien I only every saw his body briefly, and always at night-time, with the curtains drawn.

This man or boy was so helpless - so beautiful.

And I was so powerful. Maybe this is what Nina feels every day.

As I stroked his body, it felt natural to dance. So, I danced slowly in front of him and around him again. This time I used my hands to touch him.

His face turned and his mouth opened in shock. I turned around and Nina stood there, her face full of contempt. She snatched a riding crop from the rack and hit him with it.

Percy shuddered, but Nina continued: *slash, slash, slash.*

I saw tears well up in his eyes as he yelled: "No, please! No more!"

I did not want that. I would have never done that. "Nina!" I cried.

Nina stepped back for a moment, and I impulsively rushed to Percy's side, throwing my arms around his quivering body.

"Angelique," she hissed, "get away from him."

I ignored her command and continued to hug him. I struggled to loosen the chain on one of his wrists, and his released arm immediately sought refuge around my body.

Nina continued to use the riding crop, hitting his body with it. After many more searing blows, she sneered: "Cowards," and she stormed from the room.

I cried softly, not so much for myself as for the pathetic figure shackled in front of me. I hastened to unchain him.

His whole body, which I had loved so much, was a mass of blood-red welts.

He sobbed quietly.

Then he spoke for the first time since his ordeal: "May I see you again?"

"No, Percy. Never try to do this sort of thing again - it is not good for you."

"I must see you," he whispered. "I must talk to you - I need *desperately* to talk to you. I cannot live without it."

I remember Nina telling me about not having relationships with slaves, but I told him I would give him my telephone number. This satisfied him, and he left quickly without a further word.

Forgetting that Nina had told me there would be three slaves, I went upstairs to look for her. I found her sat in the living room next to the fire.

It felt natural to sit at her feet.

## CHAPTER FIFTEEN

Nina handed me a glass - I drank it in one gulp.
It was vodka.

Without a word, she handed me a second,
then a third. Soon I was warm inside, and my
mind was free of any hesitations.

I leant on Nina's legs, caressing them with
one hand and taking glass after glass of vodka
with the other.

Nina placed a long Russian cigarette in my
mouth and lit it with a match. As it flared, I
looked again into her beautiful eyes.

"Why did you whip him, Nina? He was so
young - so handsome."

"Why did you whip him, Angelique? He
was so old and helpless."

"I don't know. He beat girls."

"Yes, he did. Despicable creature.
Disgusting. Do you hear that Morley!" she
shouted.

"Come on. There is one more."

Nina grabbed me and pulled me up. I felt

dizzy and unsteady on my feet. Nina led me back down to the basement.

She flicked a switch on a wall and then went to the one of the end curtains, which Nina pulled back.

A red spot-light shone down, illuminating the ugly creature of a man, chained on a stool in such a fashion as to exhibit his ugliest parts.

I felt sick.

His head, devoid of hair, was like a misshapen and enormous egg, with a pair of little pig-like eyes and a coarse slit full of rotten teeth.

His arms and legs had no shape, and just seemed to be stuck to his obese body. His bum and mouth were no more than slits around rolls of fat.

"Look, Morley - I promised you a lovely, blonde virgin. What do you think of her, after all those strawberry-blonde tarts you have been played for a sucker by in New York? Look, Morley, you do not have to travel to Taiwan and around the East looking for virgins. Look, Morley, she is yours - all you have to do is submit to the punishment I choose to impose on you."

His slit of a mouth twisted into a smile as Nina spoke.

I felt light-headed.

Nina continued to hiss at him; "Would you like to make love to her?"

"Yes," came his reply, through rotten teeth.

The image of him on top of me flashed through my mind. I felt sick.

Then, I thought of Percy. Well, if I hadn't been able to finish my dance for Percy, I would finish it for Morley, just to torture him.

I began to dance.

I danced closer and closer to his perspiring carcass, twisting and gyrating as I moved in.

I pushed my breasts close to his face, close to his open and dribbling mouth.

I loved the feeling of power.

My body and my mind were melting into one, and it was a fantastic feeling.

"Morley, would you like to have her all to yourself?" said Nina.

"Yes!" he cried.

*Whack.*

Nina laid the first blow with her whip. Morley shuddered.

"Morley, would you leave your wife and your children again, if you could have her?"

Before he answered, I knew what he would say. Men were useless animals with no feeling and no understanding. I now enjoyed the feeling of power I had over this creature - it was more than he deserved. When I saw him, I saw Damien.

Before Morley could reply, he received two more whacks.

He finally answered: "Yes", but his voice was a little weaker than before. Still, every answer he gave angered me.

I would torture him by teasing him with my body, whilst Nina would torture him with pain.

I walked over to him and pushed my corselet up to his face, so that my covered breasts were inches from him.

I could smell his foul breath, and it made me gag.

Nina came up behind me and began whipping him more and more. As Nina's blows grew more violent, Morley's quivering increased. Then, whilst whipping him with her right hand, she used her left hand to drop a red veil around my neck and over my body.

"Kiss her Morley," she murmured. "Look: she is so close to you."

Then she unzipped my corselet and threw it to the floor, leaving me completely naked, except for the veil.

This was the first time I had been naked in front of any man except Damien and it was in front of this disgusting creature. Still I continued to punish him with my dancing.

I ran my hands over my body. I felt my breasts, I felt my nipples, I felt my stomach and I felt my pussy.

I stood up, sweat glistening on my body, and stepped over to Morley.

The sweat on my naked body glistened in the red lights.

I bent down and looked at him closely. My hair touched his head.

He stared at my breasts, inches from his face. My nipples were so erect and so close to his mouth, I could feel his breath on them.

I knew if he wasn't shacked he could grab them easily, and they were so small they would fit in the palm of his hand.

I could feel it building in my body: the heat between my legs.

Then the idea - the danger.

I stood up and with my back to him, so that he could see my rear.

I bent forwards away from him, opening my rear up to him.

Then I spread my legs. I could feel myself getting wet, but I could not stop.

I knew that he could clearly see the lips of my pussy.

On the floor, I slowly closed my legs, and bent my waist forward.

The pressure and touch of my legs coming together was too much. I tried to stop myself by holding my breath, but I couldn't stop.

I let out a moan as I came.

I rose up, feeling giddy and unsteady on my feet.

I turned around and looked at Morley, who was grinning like a pig.

There was no part of my body he had not seen.

I had an idea to take the stupid grin off his face.

I walked over to the back door of the basement where the curtain was. I pulled it down and brought it to Nina.

"Let us wrap him in that, and then put him in the tool house out in the garden," I said.

Nina broke into a wild laugh.

"See this, Morley? This is what you get for being so disgusting. No more games."

First she unchained him, then she threw the curtain over him and wrapped the pull-string around his feet, so he was completely helpless.

I exploded into mad laughter as I looked at this ridiculous figure.

I danced around him with glee as we led

him out the back door, down the garden path
and put him in the tool-house.

## CHAPTER SIXTEEN

The bright sun disturbed me as I lay on my bed, wondering how I got there.

I started counting the spots of light on the ceiling, which kept getting larger and larger, until they grew into faces staring down at me.

What had happened to my mind? How did I get here? Nina - where was she?

I rolled over and buried my face in the pillow to get away from those leering eyes of the faces.

I pressed my fingers onto my eyelids to make beautiful flickering stars. The harder I pressed, the more colours flashed before my brain.

The phone rang.

The ringing hurt my head. Nina's voice soothed the ache;

"I would love to be with you today. I like to drive to my cottage, so I'll pick you up. We could swim and relax in the sun. We could take my boat and dream on the water. I'll cook for you.

You will have to bring nothing - all is provided for."

"What is a cottage?" I said, confused.

"A cottage is a little house by the lake," she said. "It is very isolated - we could swim in the nude."

"I would love to see your cottage, Nina. I just need bit of time to pull myself together. I am not so sure what happened to me and how I got here."

"Don't worry, my darling. Take your time. I will pick you up in an hour - is that enough?"

I said yes, and she hung up.

I wondered whether I was in love with Nina.

## CHAPTER SEVENTEEN

Nina looked amazing in her white tank top and white trousers. She wore no shoes. Her large breasts made her waist look tiny.

"Take this scarf," she said, "and cover your hair and ears. It will be quite windy in the convertible."

When we were on the highway, I asked her what happened to the old man.

"He is actually not that old - about sixty-eight. His wife passed away when his only daughter was about five, and he brought her up alone.

"He beat her for the slightest misdemeanours. He thought that was the thing to do. The gym teacher noticed some marks, and the girl was taken away by *Children's Aid*. But the girl always asked to be returned to her father, explaining that she had indeed behaved very terribly. This went on and on over the years. *Children's Aid* and foster homes, then back to daddy again. When she was sixteen, she ran away. He tried everything to find her. He had ads in the paper, and since he was quite well-off, he had private-eyes out looking for her. They never found her. The investigators detected that she had obtained a passport and left Canada. That was the end of the trail."

"So, what he wants is to actually suffer the fate his girl suffered? To experience the pain she experienced?"

"Waiting chained and imagining what punishment is to come seems to be what he wants, rather than the actual lashing. I often think that a psychologist could help him more."

"Perhaps he needs a doctor."

"I also told him that donating to an orphanage or volunteering would be a better cure. He prefers to torture himself."

"And what about Percy? Why did you beat him up that viciously?" I asked.

"Percy was a one-time scenario. His mother is from Afghanistan, and she was forced into marriage when she was fourteen years old. An aunt helped her escape to Canada.

"They had a cat and a dog, but he disliked animals, so he never bothered to feed them or care for them.

"When he was twenty-one and in university, the mother had to return to her homeland to see

her ailing parents one more time, and he was
charged with taking care of the animals. It was
just a matter of ten days.

"When she returned, she found that the cat
and the dog were locked in the basement and
had not eaten for ten days. They barely survived,
by licking water from a dripping pipe. She took
them to the vet, and he nursed them back to
health in his clinic. So, his mother asked me to
punish her son with forty lashes."

"Don't you think that is unusual? What
mother would do that?"

"She had received that treatment when she
refused to marry at fourteen. She also told me
that she cannot get through to him that beating
up girls, such as he witnessed in other Afghan
families, is not the right thing to do.

"He seems to think that girls have to submit
by force. His mother also wanted him to know
what it feels like to be whipped. You know his
mother was upstairs with my husband."

'My God,' I thought, 'this is so unbelievably
unusual.' I was not sure if I wanted to hear about
Morley, the third slave.

Nina knew my thoughts: "Don't even think
about Morley, Angelique. He is a pig, a swine
and a glutton. He does not care about his own
body. He has not even got the guts to go to a

dentist. He deserves to be beaten every day. The kind of men that travel the world in search of fifty-dollar virgins are the worst types. I despise them, and I hold him in contempt. If I could, I would flog him so hard that he could never abuse women again. He is a masochist and a sadist. Any man who can do this to young girls should be jailed or shot, or at least tortured. I let him have it when I can. It will take quite some time for him to recover, but he will be back. Don't talk about Morley - he makes me sick."

Nina's cottage was built into a hillside, surrounded by trees, and not visible from the side road. It was unlocked. It was all wood, surrounded by white.

I had never seen anything so beautiful.

Nina marched into the bedroom, and emerged only with a white towel to cover her.

"Come on – let's swim."

We walked across the meadow and down to the beach. Nina walked ahead to the water's edge, stopped and dropped her towel.

I just stared.

The sun silhouetted the rear of her body, like a work of art against the water.

Just the outline of her body, with her perfect curves, was beautiful to me.

Nina jumped into the water before shouting for me to join her.

I wanted to be with her.

I had lost my inhibitions of being naked in front of Nina, so I undressed and walked over to the water.

It felt freezing.

Nina turned and stepped out of the water to meet me.

This was the first time I had seen her naked.

From her long neck, to her round shoulders, to her slim, toned arms, down her flat stomach and down to her thighs, there was not an ounce of fat on her body. Beneath her skin I could see the firm tone of her muscles.

Her breasts stood out, looking huge on her slim body.

Nina looked like Aphrodite stepping out of the water for the first time, after being created from Zeus's seed. I wondered if that was what she was - a goddess.

Nina stared at me and took my hands.

As I stepped into the water, goose-pimples ran over body.

Nina continued to lead me into the water.

As it got deeper and deeper, we got closer and closer, until I felt her nipples press against my breast.

I continued stepping towards her.

Nina just stared into my eyes.

Our breasts pressed against each other.

I wanted to be closer still.

Nina bit her lip and smiled.

Then she raised her arms, pushed me back in the water and splashed me.

I splashed her back.

For the next hour we just played in the water. To me, it was like nothing else existed - there was nowhere else I would have rather have been, than there with Nina.

Afterwards, we both stretched out on our towels on the beach, and enjoyed the sun.

"Tell me about yourself, Nina. I told you everything about Dad, about Damien, about my life. How did you grow up? What happened to you when you were young? I know nothing at all about you."

"Okay, Angelique, I will tell you a story... I grew up in Russia - once, when I was a kid, I got some money to go shopping, and I lost it; somehow I lost it on the way, so I came home with no food. I got a terrible beating.

"I went out again to look for the money, and I searched every little area I had walked. Surprisingly, I found it! Happily, I went back home and gave it to my mother, and there I got a beating again, only this time much worse.

"She claimed that I had only hidden it. Does that make sense to you?"

I didn't know what to say. I had never been beaten before - I couldn't understand it.

"It makes very little sense to me," I said.

"I shouted and screeched at my Mum that I had searched for the money for an hour, and after she had beaten me black and blue with my father's belt, she felt sorry and took me into her arms, kissing me gently. Oh, Angelique... what bliss."

"Did you love your parents?"

"No. I simply didn't understand my mother: she beat me, she kissed me, and my father did not care. My life was hell - that is all I can say - with poverty and wolves at the door."

"Real wolves came to your door?"

"It's a saying, darling: it means 'penniless'. Later, when I ran away from home at fourteen, I walked for miles and miles, just to get food.

"But, guess what: there was no man that would help a starving fourteen-year old-girl - they wanted me to *perform* for them first. In truth, they would have taken what they wanted, whether they gave me food or not.

"Some of the farmers did it seven times with

me before they fed me. But how wonderful it was then, to be warm and secure and fed. How can I explain it, that canopy of heaven, to sleep in a warm bed after being raped seven times..? Does that make sense?"

"It is a nightmare, Nina, and very difficult to understand. I can't imagine a life like that."

"When I got married, I married a Polish construction worker. He was very tough, and that's really what I liked. Honestly."

"How old were you then?"

"Oh, I was about seventeen. I used to work in a laundry shop. This particular shop was bombed one night, but all the girls got out in time. When my husband came into the bunker underground, I told the girls that they should tell him I was dead, but I was just hiding behind a corner."

"Why would you do that?"

"You know what seventeen year olds do - really stupid, ignorant things. My husband's face was snow-white.

"Then I came around the corner and laughed, and I waited for him to laugh - it was a joke. But you know what he did? He beat me. Right in front of all the girls. He grabbed me by the hair, took a stick and beat me with it. He beat every part of my body he could: my arms, my legs, my body and my back. The girls just stared, since they could not run away in the bunker. Then he took me into his arms and hugged me and kissed me. He picked me up and carried me in his arms. As he kissed me and loved me, he said: 'Oh, my darling, that you live!' I was so very happy - does that make any sense?"

"Your behaviour was very cruel, Nina: he thought you were dead. I can understand his feelings when he saw you alive, but his actions were very irrational. It is so strange to imagine that you got beaten, but, strangely, you felt like you were at a place of bliss - *heaven*, as you say. It is strange."

"It is hard to understand. You are still a teenager and I am over forty."

"What happened to your husband?"

"He beat me and raped me whenever it pleased him. I ran away. The husband I have right now is civilized - he won't beat me. Whatever I do, he won't lay a hand on me."

"But he approves of what you do? I mean: your business and the slaves?"

Nina's gaze darkened. Then she smiled.

"He has no choice, does he? I do what I like to do, and nobody, but nobody, will tell me what I can and cannot do, most certainly not a man. I may occasionally listen to a woman's advice."

I was so stunned I could not say or do anything but stare at her. I could not possibly imagine a life like that, and I felt so sorry for her. I wish I was older than her - I wish I could have been there, so I could have looked after her and protected her. I just wanted to hug her and kiss her.

Then I thought: 'Perhaps she would only want me to beat her.' And I felt sad.

## CHAPTER EIGHTEEN

Two weeks had gone by, and we were at the cottage again. We arrived late, slept until the afternoon, and now that the weather was fantastic, we had breakfast outside on the balcony.

Still, as we ate, Nina looked withdrawn. She was hardly speaking, and not touching her food.

"I am on the run," Nina said.

"What do you mean?"

"I am on the run, and I do not even know what I am running from, or where I am running to. I am going on a cruise around the world."

"Really? Wow. That sounds like a dream."

"A dream? So you think that would be a dream? Would it be again a love affair, like on my last boat trip? Another officer, drunk full-time, but very charming? Into his bed and out again? Then I would return to my 'sin pool' to earn my living: something 'special' and extraordinary. Something 'special', with the steady fear that the police would catch me doing it. But what else can I do? Nothing!"

"Are you really afraid of the police?"

She shrugged her shoulders, and raised her elbows onto the table. She raised her hands and encircled her face. Then she looked at me very seriously, and said: "My husband is trying to vet all these slaves very carefully, and I am extremely careful myself, but things can happen, and believe me, this activity is not exactly appreciated by the police force."

I was shocked, and suddenly realised that I had never considered this eventuality.

"I love men, Angelique. I *adore* them basically... basically... Yet I am still waiting for the one to come along. At forty I am still waiting for the one who will take me and drive me far, far away to some wonderland that does not exist. But, instead of the Prince Charming, they come for a lashing. Out of every ten men, there are eight who want more than just the whip. That's what I've learned, so that's what I do."

"But you are the master: you can do everything you like."

"After a while they all despise me for my service, and they still come again and again. I do not despise them because of their need. Naturally they can't have it at home, so they go somewhere else, but why do they despise me? I am the one that gives them satisfaction, talks to them, listens to their disturbed minds. I am the only one that ever listens to them in their loneliness and desperation, so why am I to be despised? I do not know."

Tears were in her eyes. She picked up a cigarette and had to try several times to light it, her hands were shaking so much.

"I want to go on the world cruise. You see, once in a while I would like to pay for the services I require, rather than being paid for my services."

I got up and walked around the table, put her face in both my hands, and said: "I always wanted a girlfriend like you: someone beautiful - a woman to adore and love and look up to. I am so glad I found you. I think you are the most spectacular woman I have ever met. You are a princess and a queen, and I only wish that one day I could be as fantastic - as successful - as you are. I have never had a friend like you. Please, never leave me."

She took my hands, kissed the knuckles, and she smiled.

"You are alone, my little dove - all alone in Canada. This is why you feel the way you feel right now. I will never leave you. You are my friend, and friends are very hard to come by."

"Thank you, Nina," I said.

Then Nina stood up. "Let's live," she declared; "Let's go dancing to great music, and live. Life is beautiful! I am so stupid, Angelique – don't listen to me: I am just an imbecile. Tonight we will have our own personal party - we will dance, we will drink, we will eat wonderful food, and if we are really lucky, we will find love for the night."

With that, Nina walked in to her bedroom and to her walk-in closet, and undressed.

I followed her in. It was like a boutique store, filled with clothes and shoes, coats and sweaters.

"Have a look here," she said; "We are about the same height, but you will have a problem with my waist, so slip into these dresses without a bra and without knickers. I put some powder onto your body, so that way you can slip into the dress easily."

"I think you have a problem with me wearing underwear, Nina," I said.

"Having no knickers and no bra is much sexier – you'll feel very liberated. Look at me." Then Nina stood back, with her robe on the floor. I looked at her again. I looked at her legs. I looked at her pussy.

"You prefer to see me with underwear on?"

I shook my head.

"Good," she said. "Now powder my body well."

After I had powdered her body, she did the same to me, and I got dressed.

I wore a red, ankle-length, Japanese-style cocktail dress, with a high collar around my neck, and slits running beyond my waist on both sides of my legs - it was very tight.

"Tonight we are hunting! We will assess the men like cattle!"

We went to the only club in town. Still, it was very classy and I loved the music. It was around ten p.m., and the place was really busy, full of people.

We had barely entered the building and we were already mobbed by men. They asked us to dance and they asked us if we wanted drinks.

We danced with them all. After every dance, we discussed the guys and assessed them, and while we were whispering in each other's ears they came again, supplying us with drinks. We kept on dancing.

I could not stop smiling and laughing with Nina. It was such good fun. This was probably the first time I had been to a club like this.

When one o'clock came around, I told Nina that there was just nobody I felt attracted to, and she felt the same.

"Give me half an hour," said Nina; "Just keep on dancing, and I will be back."

I looked at her, but she just shook her head and disappeared.

After forty-five minutes, she returned. "I found two guys," she said; "have a look – I'm sure you'll like them."

"And if I don't?"

"Oh, you will: one looks just like Geoffrey - you can have him. And since he isn't a slave, you can fuck him or let him fuck you."

We both stepped out of the club, and there they were.

He was very good looking. And he did look like Geoffrey, only younger.

Nina told the men to go to their hotel and we would follow them in our car.

When I was alone with her she handed me two condoms and said: "Take these. The silver one will make you feel really good. We are just two rooms apart in the hotel. I will come and get you in the morning, okay?"

And so, we drove back to their hotel.

We had some drinks, smoked a few cigarettes, and then we danced in the bar, even though we were the only people there.

I had consumed many drinks, but my heart

was beating so fast that I thought I would have a
heart-attack.

I thought of Damien. I had only ever made
love to him. 'How I hate him,' I thought. He had
probably fucked ten women by now. I would
fuck the man I was with - I would fuck the man
who looked like Geoffrey.

The man saw me shivering and leant over to
rub my arms. Then he rubbed my face and
kissed me. I kissed him back. Then he took my
hand and led me to his hotel room.

Inside the door he put his hands on my
waist and kissed the back of my neck. Then he
turned me around and again kissed me.

I kissed him back and put my hands on his
body, whilst he kissed my neck.

I felt my nipples getting hard.

He pulled the top of my dress down and
took my nipples in his mouth. He kissed them
softly. Then he sucked them hard.

He kissed and sucked my body like I was
the first female he had ever seen.

He only broke off kissing me to remove his
clothes. Although he was slightly older than me -
about twenty-five - he had the toned body of an
eighteen-year old; I marvelled at it.

He led me over to the bed and gently
pushed me down. Then he turned on the little

light on the table next to the bed and pulled off my dress, down over my legs.

"You're beautiful… you're beautiful…" he said, before kissing me on the mouth again.

I could feel his huge erection pressing against my legs.

I was wet just thinking about it being inside me.

He kissed me down my neck, over my breasts and down my stomach. It tickled and I had to stifle a giggle. He looked up, smiled and then continued to kiss his way down.

The kisses stopped when he reached between my legs.

I lay there, too shy to look at him. I just stared at the ceiling. I was so happy. I wondered what he would do next.

Then I felt his breath running over my pussy.

I was already wet and I felt a shiver travel up my body.

I felt the tip of his tongue touch me for a split second. Then I felt it again, slightly longer this time. Then I felt it stroking and licking me.

As this man put his tongue inside me, I lost count of the time.

I couldn't breathe - I felt dizzy. My head began to spin, and my whole body erupted in a wave.

Jesus.

Wow.

Then he was kissing me on the mouth again.

I could taste my sex on his lips.

Then his hardness between my legs.

Unlike my first time with Damien, I was not worried about it hurting, or whether I would enjoy it. I knew I would love it, and love this man doing it.

I gasped as his hard penis entered me.

I have never felt something like this.

I lost my breath again, just as he kissed me.

Over and over again he thrust into me.

I lost my mind.

I couldn't think.

I wanted to touch him.

I placed my hands on his arms and felt his muscles tense, as he continued to enter me.

It was harder and harder to breathe.

I put my hands on his bum and opened my legs wider for him, as he thrust into me.

I wanted him deeper.

I wanted him harder.

I wanted him to come inside me.

Then I felt my body shudder again, as another wave hit me.

Wow.

Again.

Jesus.

My head.

My body.

It just tingles. I need to get my breath back.

I just lay there, whilst the man lay next to me, looking at and stroking my body.

Then he kissed me again.

This man made love to me all night.

I may have drifted away for a few minutes here and there, but that was it.

I was still in bed with him when Nina opened the door.

I kissed him lightly on the cheek and thanked him for an amazing time. He just smiled, thanked me and kissed me on the cheek back.

As we walked away, I told Nina: "He was only my second man, Nina. Did you know that?"

She smiled. "Your life has started again, my darling. Now you can forget the past and live."

When we reached the outside of the hotel, the sun was already up and people were already going to work. We both had shadows under our eyes. Several people stared at us as we walked back to the car.

"Oh, how would people judge us?!" said

Nina. "We are a bunch of very bad women: psychopaths, absolutely crazy! To make love, to have sex and to fuck a man! What madness!"

In the car, Nina continued as we drove back to the cottage:

"I wonder why a woman is looked down upon for loving a stranger. But when a man does it, he is adored, and even boasts about it with other men, even though he may be married. Has a woman not the same right? I wonder why we are constantly berated. It makes no sense to me."

## CHAPTER NINETEEN

Nina did not say anything as we arrived at the cottage.

She got undressed, closed the curtains and got into bed.

I pulled off my dress and followed her in.

I lay close to her, on my side, just watching her stare up at the ceiling.

I kissed her cheek.

I kissed her neck.

I planted three little kisses down her shoulders.

Her skin was so soft, so beautiful.

I loved her very much.

I reached out with my hand and placed it on her stomach.

Her eyes were closed and she did not respond.

I moved closer and kissed her neck, and then her shoulder again.

Then I rested my head on her breast and just lay there, listening to her breathing until I fell

ANGELIQUE MANON

asleep.

## CHAPTER TWENTY

"Do you like this apartment?" asked Nina, as she sat on the floor in my apartment, her back to the sofa.

"Yes, of course," I replied, looking around.

"Nonsense: it's too small for you. There's not enough room in here even to hang a slave. You need somewhere bigger."

If it hadn't been Nina saying this, I would have thought that she was joking.

"Nina, I can't afford to live anywhere else."

"You know what I think about money," said Nina.

I nodded.

"Well, the job you have does not suit you. We could make a pact."

"A what?"

"A pact."

"Like a deal?" I asked.

"A deal is good, but a pact is even better," she replied. "A pact where we both provide each other with something equal in value, for me to

123

give to you."

I really had no idea what Nina was talking about.

"Nina, I have nothing to give to you of any value. I really don't know what you mean."

She smiled - that wicked smile.

"Your time, your beauty and your charm - those are things of value. They are of value to me and of value to my slaves. I will provide you with a much bigger and nicer apartment than this, in downtown Toronto."

"Nina, there is no way I could accept that."

"In return I want three things from you."

"What?"

"The first thing I want is for you to drive me every fourteen days up to the cottage, and stay with me for the weekend."

I couldn't think of anything I'd rather do more than stay with Nina. I would never leave her at all, if she would allow it.

"Of course. What are the other two?"

"The second thing is: I want you to drive to see me, even in the winter-time."

"Yes, Nina. What's the third thing?"

"The third thing is that I want you take ten slaves from me."

"What? Nina, are you joking? How am I supposed to deal with ten slaves. I just about have time now with work."

"I've said: the job doesn't suit you, or me. You will leave your job. You will not need to pay for the apartment and you will be rewarded by each and every slave that you see. Like I told you, I do not think nor worry about money, and you will not have to either."

"I asked you to be serious, and I'm not sure if you are."

"I am deadly serious. Nothing would please me more. You would be doing me a favour by taking my slaves from me, as I have too many already."

"Nina, I can't leave my job: I need to give notice."

"No. I will speak with Dan and tell him you are not coming in any more and he will make sure that your boss is fully compensated for their understanding."

"Nina, I am not sure."

"We need a schedule. A schedule to arrange the days that you will see your slaves. You need to allow enough time for you to properly prepare yourself and your environment for each slave. Do you have paper?"

"What now? You want to do the schedule now?"

"There is no time to waste, my darling."

I stood up, went to the kitchen and fetched a writing pad and a black fountain pen.

Nina took the pad and began writing down my schedule. The more she wrote on the page, the more I fretted.

"Nina, please, I don't think I can do this. It's too much."

"Most people waste their time when they are young and have the energy to do things," she said, raising her voice. "You are young now - you have the energy and the brains, so don't waste a minute of your valuable time. You can do it!"

One piece of paper after the other flew into the garbage as Nina scrawled down a timetable. It took us more than four hours to complete. When it was finished it was like a masterpiece: every minute of my time had been accounted for.

Nina promised to help me every step of the way.

Two weeks later, Nina arranged for me to move into my new apartment; it was on Jameson Avenue - a very nice part of Toronto.

I couldn't believe it when I first stepped inside: it was huge and so elegant - the type of apartment I had seen in movies.

It was also nicely furnished, but I knew it

would need to change, as I prepared it to start accepting my slaves.

On the day I moved in Nina came with me, and brought a picnic basket and a bottle of Champagne to celebrate.

"Let's have a picnic here and celebrate your newfound freedom." Nina opened up the basket and produced some cheese, grapes, crackers, orange juice and a small tablecloth. She set the table with little orange cups, saucers, and plates. She had matching knives, forks, and spoons, all made of orange plastic, and two red roses that she placed in a vase.

After we had eaten, we sat on my new bed, smoked, and drank Champagne.

"Do you know the difference between a dominant female and a domineering female?" she asked.

"They are both the same," I answered.

"No, they are not. Let me tell you what a 'dominant' female is like: it is a woman who is aware of the physiological fact that in a sexual relationship the maximum pleasure for both can only be attained if the female retains absolute control of the sex act."

I considered her words carefully. I thought about what had happened in my life so far, and about Damien. "It doesn't work like that for me,

Nina, because I have never controlled anything."

"You controlled the slaves I gave you. No?"

"You are right there, but as you have said before: we don't have sex with our slaves, so they do not count. I know that if I was with a man other than a slave, I could not be assertive or have any control at all."

"You are correct in relation to the men that are your slaves, and this is a danger I have and will continue to warn you about. But in general, Angelique, with other men, when you find a new relationship is what I am speaking of. There is no tyranny of a woman over a man here - there is merely the fulfilment of nature's arrangement: the female animal leads and guides the male animal to a climax by controlling the whole proceeding, so as to bring about mutual fulfilment of both in the union."

"In the animal world, perhaps. Yes, in the animal world, but it is hard to see that between a man and a woman."

Nina sighed: "Angelique, I see I have to be patient here. Consider the following: are we not animals? Are the male organs such that they have no mystery about them whatsoever, as they hang crudely dangling, for all to see."

"Yes."

"Look at your organs: they are completely

concealed within the recesses of the female form."

"Yes."

"The female is therefore the source of all mystery, and the male is accordingly entirely dependent upon the female for this power."

"But I did not have control or power over Damien, or the man in the hotel. And you have said many times that for total erotic enjoyment, the female must be the master and the male the slave. But, Nina, we have no sex with our slaves, so I am afraid I cannot agree. No... I do not agree-"

Nina slapped her hand down on the side.

"Jesus, Angelique! Sometimes it is frustrating to have a conversation with you. I get baffled - I almost feel defeated."

I was taken aback by her voice - she had never spoken to me like this before. I had never seen her angry.

"I am sorry. I really don't want to make you angry. I truly didn't understand the difference between a dominant woman and a domineering one."

Nina took a deep breath. "Angelique, the great distinction is that the domineering woman exercises her tyranny for the sole purpose of satisfying herself, without participating in acts which she considers sinful. The dominant female, however, develops her power for the purpose of enriching the enjoyment of both herself and her male partner in the act of love."

Nina did not shout again, but I could tell she was still angry with me. When she had finished speaking, she looked out of the window.

It was almost dark.

She stood up, said one final thing to me and then left.

I stood on the balcony and looked down, and I watched her climb into her car and drive off.

I couldn't understand what had happened.

I went into the bathroom, looked into the mirror and stared at my reflection - my tears had made my make-up run.

"You made her angry today," I said to myself. "She was frustrated. What did you do that for? How can you make her angry after everything she has done for you?"

I felt my chest getting heavy and my eyes welling. I sat down on the floor and began to cry. I thought about Mum and Dad, my sisters... my lovely family. My biggest mistake, I thought, was that I interrupted and I did not listen. My Dad told me again and again that I had to listen to his patients and that I constantly interrupted;

"Listening is gold - talking is silver." These had been Nina's words as well.

I cried again. I cried more than I had cried when I was in Paris.

After a while I began to feel the coldness of the floor on my bum and legs. I pulled myself up using the sink, looked in the mirror again and saw my tear-stained reflection. I took toilet roll and began to wipe the streaked make-up off my face.

I thought to myself: 'I need to listen more carefully. I should write down what she said. I should consider it very carefully. She is wise - *so* wise – and I have so much to learn.' I sat down, and I wrote from memory what she said before she left.

"You can develop into a very beautiful, dominant female."

## CHAPTER TWENTY-ONE

"Would you like to see Lisa again?" said Nina one night. "There is a party, and I would love to go."

"Will Geoffrey be there?"

"No, but Dan will be there, as well as quite a few of my slaves. I would like you to meet them, especially as you will be taking them. I would like to wear a very special dress for the occasion. I saw a dress at 'The Room' in the Simpsons store - it is made of black lace; it has an undergarment like a silk slip, with very thin straps. I would like us to attend looking like twin sisters, wearing the same dress."

We went shopping the next day. When we arrived at the Simpsons store, the sales-lady almost ran to greet Nina, escorted us to a VIP room at the top floor and arranged for a waitress to bring us drinks. She then asked Nina if we would like a model to wear the dresses.

"Why do I need a model when I have this

exquisite creature with me? Angelique will try on the dresses."

"Of course," said the woman, who then hurried off.

The lady came back ten minutes later carrying two different, but near-identical dresses - both were like Nina had described.

I looked at them all, but there was only one I really liked.

The dress was very elegant. It had long arms, and the lace fell lightly upon the hands. It had a high neck - so high that the lace completely concealed the neck and framed the face, like petals around an open flower.  Light like a feather, it fell over the black slip and was very comfortable. It looked regal.

It was the most gorgeous dress I had ever seen, but I could not help noticing the price tag. Although I was used to Nina giving me money and buying me things, with this I felt it was too much.

"Do you like it?" asked Nina.

"Of course I like it! But only millionaires could afford it."

"We'll take these two dresses," Nina said to the sales-lady, "and don't forget the two evening purses I selected, with the black pearls. And bring the two pairs of shoes - we would like to try them on."

I looked at Nina. I was sure that she loved me like I loved her.

"You are my daughter, and daughters never say no to their mothers. Don't you know that?"

The two pairs of pumps were made of black silk, and they were covered with little rhinestones, as if sprinkled with diamonds. I had never seen such shoes before, and they were amazingly comfortable, despite the fact that they had stiletto heels.

The two purses were made with black pearls, and the claps, too, bore rhinestones that glittered like diamonds. They were small, but very heavy for their size.

"Stay there," said Nina; "I'll be back in a minute." She walked away with the sales-lady and returned minutes later with two shopping bags. She handed me one and we walked out.

When we were back in the car, she said: "Look, Angelique, there are just a few things I enjoy in my life, and today was one day I truly enjoyed. When I see you with this dress at the party, then I will be happy. So, please just let me be happy, okay?"

"Thank you, Nina. I will feel like a princess."

"You are *my* little princess," she said, "and I love you."

"But do you love me like a princess, or like a sister, or like a daughter or a husband?"

"I love you Angelique, and that is all you need to ask and all you need to hear."

Again, after such a high, trying on and receiving such a beautiful outfit, I felt down. It was not what I wanted to hear: I wanted Nina to love me like a lover.

I thought about Lisa. "Tell me about Lisa: do you love her?"

"I like her alot. We've been friends for many years."

"But you don't love her like you love me?"

"I don't love anyone like I love you, Angelique."

I smiled. This felt special to me.

"But, you know, even though she is a good friend of mine, I do not see her as much as I would wish. You see, Lisa has to lay a bit low: she had some trouble with the vice."

"Vice? What is this?"

"The vice squad - the cops."

"What happened?"

"She has a massage business, and I guess she massaged some parts on a man's body you aren't supposed to massage."

Even though Angelique had mentioned about the police before, it was not a danger I always thought about. But this worried me. "Could the vice ever come after you?" I asked.

"As I have said before: the danger of the vice is a danger that we all must deal with," Nina laughed. "Of course, you will never utter a word, will you - this is just between you and me?"

"Is Lisa a dominant female or a domineering female?"

"Unfortunately, Lisa is domineering and she had a strong man. He did not put up with that shit, hence she is now divorced.

"I will teach you how to control men - how to dominate them without being domineering. Then, Angelique, you will be happy."

We drove back to my apartment and tried on the dress and the shoes. We both looked in the mirror.

"You look so gorgeous," Nina said. "I have just the man for you: Michael will be the perfect subject to start you off with in this exciting adventure - the exercise of female power - because he believes in the things I told you about the other evening. He accepts the truth of female power and knows that the symbol of that power can be the whip. He is what I would call an *erotic masochist*."

When Nina picked me up to drive to the

party, she looked so striking that I could not stop looking at her. For the first time, she wore make-up and her face looked like a painting; a face so immaculate, so absolutely gorgeous, that I realised she was much more beautiful than I could ever be.

"Why don't you model?" I asked. "Why don't you go to an agency and apply for a modelling job? They would take you immediately. I know it."

She smiled. "Thank you very much, but no. Besides, nobody would hire a forty-year-old woman - your chances are by far better than mine."

We pulled up outside Lisa's house. Nina turned to me and said: "When I pinch you, then you know that the man I am speaking to is a slave of mine."

We went up to the house and were greeted by Lisa; she had a radiant smile on her face - so different than the first welcome I had received from her.

"Oh, my God - look at you two! You look like sisters." She smiled and gave us each a hug.

She led us into the living room and personally introduced me to a few men and women I had not met before.

I saw Dan again, and he kissed my hand and

said: "Oh, Angelique, you are so beautiful. Black looks so perfect with your blonde hair and your light skin. I hear you are doing very well. Don't worry about your old job: it is all taken care of."

"What about you? What are you doing?" I asked.

"The same old boring job," he said, smiling.

Nina took me and walked me around the party, sipping gin and tonic. Each time she introduced me to a man I had never met before, she pinched me, just to let me know they were one of her slaves. My skin was starting to hurt from it. I truly did not believe how there could be so many. I remembered a few of their names: 'Keith', 'Peter' and 'Rod'; none of them were particularly memorable.

Each time Nina introduced me to a man, I hoped that he would turn around and be Geoffrey, but unfortunately, as Nina had said, he was not there.

I also met Michael, who Nina had mentioned before,. and I thought he was old, and not very attractive.

"How do you like Michael?" asked Nina. "I noticed you are not impressed. I know he is a bum- Well, not really… he just *looks* like a bum."

Her last words shocked. I couldn't understand how he would be a bum and know

Nina.

Nina continued: "He is about fifty-five years of age, and you think he is old. But he had made an investment that turned out to be a mistake - he lost a modest fortune, and when this happened, his wife left him and returned to her home in the United States, taking with her their daughter, who was very much under her influence. He was left here in Canada, alone and without a penny. He was over his head in debts, and he felt that he was too old to start his business over again."

"So, what is he doing now?"

"He is in the construction business in a very small way, and as he is very clever with his hands, he could make you any instrument or equipment you need to carry out your role as an imperious female. What is more important is he will do this for you because he understands these things. If you are prepared to meet him, I am sure you will learn all about masochism, and much more."

I didn't reply immediately - I didn't know what to say. So I just looked at Nina.

"Do I need to draw you a picture, Angelique? What is wrong with you? Michael will call you," she snapped.

"I'm sorry, Nina," I said.

Nina looked at me, hugged me and we continued to walk around the party. However, compared to what had happened to me so far, it was very boring and ordinary.

A week later I met Michael.

## CHAPTER TWENTY-TWO

Michael was old and he looked his age; grey
hair, over-weight, old-fashioned clothes and he
drove a beat-up Chevrolet truck, cluttered with
dusty construction junk.

But, what fascinated me about Michael, and
what I liked about him, was that he was
unwilling to accept his financial reversal – his
fall from grace, which Nina had described as a
"final sentence of poverty" - but proceeded to do
something about it, through hard work and
sweat in the construction business.

When he talked, he talked with passion,
vision and purpose. He also spoke vividly of his
previous life, that even *I* would strive to live
now.

He also told me about his wife: a
despotically inclined matriarch. For her, sex was
something to be endured as a form of duty,
while the husband's duty was to make her life
comfortable and secure. He was her meal-ticket.
She therefore had no misgivings about leaving

him alone and broke.

One day Michael said to me: "I will start a new life in a dream world, with a beautiful, strong-willed, dominant woman, and I will place her upon a throne. In my lonely hours, I will silently worship her."

I was so taken aback that I just looked at him, unable to say anything. I understood more about what Nina had been trying to tell me.

I soon found out that in order to make Michael's dream come true, he would be willing to do anything. This, without a doubt, endeared me to him.

I wanted to turn my apartment into a place where I could host and control my slaves, but in order to do this it, would take much work.

Michael wanted to become my slave and he worked in construction, so he was the obvious person to assist me. I decided that Michael would become my first slave.

Michael worked on this project for me, hopefully, but silently - the complete opposite to how Geoffrey had been with me.

The first part of my plan was to make my apartment as soundproof as possible, and to accomplish this in a very decorative way. We covered the cracks around the apartment entrance door with flexible black rubber strips, and inside the door we hung thick, black velvet curtains, which completely covered the entrance door - Michael hung them on a track so they could be pulled back to open the door.

The arch-way between the little entrance hall and my L-shaped living room was treated similarly, with heavy, black velvet curtains, so that there was a double set of black curtains between the living room and the corridor of my bachelorette's apartment.

Only one wall of my apartment adjoined another apartment, so I had Michael build a false cork wall to make it soundproof, onto which I could place all kinds of decorations.

Then I fastened a string of little Indian brass bells on the curtains between the living room and the entrance hall. My plan was that my slave could prepare himself in the entrance hall without being able to see me, and then he could move the curtains so that the tinkling of the bells would be the signal that he was ready, without his ever speaking.

The entrance hall became a sort of bridge between the ordinary, everyday world and the special world within.

The next thing I needed was the equipment I had to have, to control my slaves and fasten them in a position that suited my whims.

I told Michael that I wanted hooks in the ceiling and floor. I smiled inwardly when I saw the expression on his face, when I said that I wanted the hooks strong enough to hang my slave upside down by the ankles.

He installed a steel bar across the opening between the living and dining areas of the L-shaped room. The bar was high up near the ceiling, and it was supported at either end by pillars. He fixed a series of hooks on the bar and on both the posts. Then, to make it decorative, I had him gild the bar and pillars, so I could hang flower baskets from it.

One evening, I had the apartment superintendent up to fix a leaking tap in the bathroom - I used this opportunity to get an impartial reaction to the appearance of my apartment.

When he had fixed the tap, I invited him to have a drink with me. He was a simple but very pleasant Greek man, and I was curious to see what he would say.

"How beautifully you have decorated your apartment! It is the nicest bachelor in the building. It is very unusual, and just a bit mysterious, or sexy."

"What do you mean by that?" I said, innocently.

He blushed: "I don't know how to explain it, but I feel extremely comfortable here. It's somehow sexy - I don't know any other word for it."

This was precisely the atmosphere I wanted.

He continued to look around.

"What's that?" he asked.

I followed his gaze, and saw that the mirrored box that Geoffrey had given me was in the corner of the room.

I blushed.

I most certainly had not moved it there. In fact, when I had moved in I had kept it hidden in one of my cupboards. So, the only person that could have was Michael, and he had done so without informing me - I was not impressed.

"Oh that is nothing - just a box-stool."

There was no need for him not to accept my answer. Neither Michael nor the superintendent knew what it truly was, but I knew that I would punish Michael for being so nosey.

Finally, I needed a whip by which I would administer the kiss of leather to my slaves. I was embarrassed, and didn't want to tell Michael that I didn't have even one whip. The problem solved itself, because one day Michael phoned me and said he had a present for me.

It was a braided leather riding crop. I will

never forget the day he brought it, or the look in his eyes as he placed it in my hand.

For days I played with it. I tried it on my own skin and was amazed at the stinging pain it brought.

Now I had everything I needed.

I was grateful for the work that Michael had done, but now it was complete I felt hesitation about taking him as a slave. I don't know if this was because I was unsure of my feelings towards him, because I felt somehow obligated to him, or because I was just nervous having to deal with a slave by myself.

I often thought about my experiences with Nina's slaves and the sessions I had attended and participated in. I realised that at that time I was really only fulfilling her orders without motivation of my own. But this experience was going to be very different, as it was going to depend on my own individual power of will.

I told Michael that I would see him as a slave, and that he should come to my apartment at the end of the week, on Friday.

I looked up at the bar in the ceiling. It was fitting that the first slave I would hang from it was the man that had assembled it.

## CHAPTER TWENTY-THREE

Michael stood alone in the entrance hall, illuminated by only red light. He could not see me through the curtain, as I lay on my sofa in a delicate, white, lace negligee.

Wagner's *"Overture of the Flying Dutchman"* played loudly, as I sat there with flutters in my stomach, waiting for myself to begin.

"Remove your clothes Michael, and put on the red slave robe that I have placed on the floor for you, where you belong."

"Yes, Angelique."

"Touch the curtains when you are done, and the bells will inform me that you are ready. I don't want to hear your voice again."

"Yes, Angelique."

I waited.

Then the bells rang.

"Stay where you are, slave, in the hallway. Sit down on the floor facing away from my voice, and cross your arms over your chest."

"Yes, Angelique."

"I said I don't want to hear your voice."

"Okay..."

I saw the movement through the curtains of him complying. I walked over with a hood I had prepared especially, and I dropped it over his head - it had a small loop on the top that dropped to his shoulders. I could now do anything I wanted, and he could not see me.

Any doubt that I had initially had about handling Michael on my own was gone - I felt excited as to what would happen.

I leaned over his shoulders and bound his arms with two straps, which fastened each wrist to the opposite elbow. As I did this, I felt his body shivering under my hands - he was breaking out in a cold sweat from nerves.

I squeezed his shoulder to reassure him. I wanted him defenceless for me, but I also wanted him to be comfortable.

I then took a tether chain and fastened it around his neck, and under the hood. I grasped the other end of the tether chain and returned to my living room to relax for a few minutes, and to allow him to contemplate his fate.

When I was ready, I took up my position in the middle of the room, where I had placed a number of very small, flaming torches, similar to the primitive ones the natives carry at night, as they walk barefoot through the jungle.

Then I picked up my bull-whip. This one was going to be a tremendous surprise for Michael, because I had acquired it without his assistance. In my other hand, I held the tether chain and a riding crop.

I was ready.

I gave the tether chain a slight tug; "Come to me, slave."

The curtain moved as Michael hobbled on across the floor towards me, struggling against his bound arms.

"Kneel on the floor, slave, and look at me."

The hood moved and looked up in my direction. I smiled. He couldn't see me.

"I am your mistress, slave. Would you like to see your new mistress and suffer the consequences?"

"Yes, mistress, I would."

*Whack.*

I struck the bull-whip down onto his back.

He cried out.

Then I lifted off his hood so he could see me.

He looked up at me, with glazed eyes and a quivering lip. Sweat ran down his forehead.

I felt power.

I felt my pussy quiver.

I began to dance around him.

His eyes followed my every move.

I wanted Michael to have an amazing experience and I wanted to shock him. I knew he had been curious about the mirrored box, so I decided to use it. I hoped it would shock him as much as it had done me.

"Lay down, slave."

He slowly lay down on the floor.

I placed the mirrored box over his head - it pressed slightly on his neck.

He began to breathe heavily.

I knew that the mirror in the base of the box would allow him to see all of his body that lay outside the stool, and he could also see a bit of the room and my legs.

"Whatever you do, slave, don't move." I took a bucket of water and placed it on top of the box. His arms were still bound, his neck was secured by the mirrored box and the weight of the bucket, and he was completely helpless.

I placed my foot onto his chest and dug my stiletto heel into him.

I knew he could see just my foot and my heel pressing against his flesh. I knew that he would be scared.

I pressed down a harder. Just a little bit more and the stiletto heel would break his skin.

I rotated my foot over his body, and as I did

I twisted my foot. His penis grew into a huge erection.

I now wished that I could see it as he did, with the mirrors in the box, it must have looked spectacular.

He began to pant and gasp.

I bent down and stroked his body with my hands, asking him if he could breathe alright.

"Yes, Mistress."

I took a bunch of feathers and caressed up and down his body for a few minutes; goose pimples erupted over his skin.

I removed the bucket.

His panting and gasping slowed.

I removed my negligee and changed into my black corselet. As I changed, he remained on the floor and did not move.

I walked over behind him and lifted the mirrored box off his head.

Then I pulled him into a sitting position and dropped the hood back on his head.

He sat there quietly, covered in sweat, but now his erection had gone. There was a small red mark around his neck where the box had been.

The music was still playing.

"Get up, slave."

Michael hobbled to his feet.

I took the chain around his neck, and led him backwards. Then I used my hands to spread his legs apart.

He began to shake.

He knew what was to come next.

I secured his ankles with chains, undid the bondage on his arms and fastened his hands to the overhead bar. Then I took off the hood.

"Which of these instruments do you think would be most severe, and which should I use on you, slave?"

He looked towards the bull-whip and riding crop.

"It's your choice," he said, quietly.

He was entirely at my mercy. I saw absolute fear in his face – for, with such instruments in front of anybody, who would not be terrified?

I stepped close to him, touched his shoulders with both my hands and whispered: "You have only to say 'red' and I will stop."

"Oh, Angelique, I adore you," he whispered; "You are like a water-nymph dancing in a deep, dark pool, your skin fragrant and dewy."

His reply shocked me and I had to step back. I wondered if he would adore me when I had finished with him. I would beat him until he said: "Red".

I began to dance.

I danced and picked up the riding crop. I moved closer and closer to Michael, until my skin-tight, black outfit touched his naked body.

*Thud.*

I hit him with the crop.

He shuddered.

*Thud.*

I hit him again.

He shuddered slightly less.

I began to hit his buttocks.

He hardly moved as I beat him. He hardly made a sound and he certainly did not say: "Red". Perhaps he really did adore me.

I dropped the riding crop, picked up the bull-whip and brought it crashing down on his back.

He let out a slight groan and shuddered again.

*Whack.*

I hit him again.

*Whack. Whack. Whack.*

I whipped his body again and again.

He did not tell me to stop, so I continued. I switched to beating his buttocks with the crop and whipping his back with the bull-whip.

Still he endured, despite bright red welts appearing over his whole body.

I picked a whip with several long lashes, and whipped him in such a way that the tips of the lashes fell upon the front of his thighs.

Tears grew in his eyes. But he still did not say: "Red".

I stopped.

I went into the bathroom, undressed and put on my white negligee. I fetched a sheet of bed linen and wrapped it around his body, leaving the arms open. I released his hands and bent down to release his ankles. I was unsure if he could stand straight, so I wrapped my arms around his body.

I felt his erection pressing against me.

I used my hands to caress his back up and down.

Michael groaned. And then he came.

"Oh, my God - I am so sorry," he said, his face becoming bright red.

"Don't be," I replied, and I hugged him harder, then kissed him on his neck. I led him to the couch and he sat down. "Listen to the music and relax. When are you are ready your clothes are in the hallway - get dressed and leave quietly."

He got up and knelt in front of me. He kissed my hand and said: "It was the most wonderful evening of my life, Angelique. Thank you."

Then he left.

I sat and smoked a cigarette, drank my Champagne and closed my eyes.

I felt like the legendary Aphrodite standing on a mountain-top, surrounded by the fire of my lightning torches.

I felt like I had conquered everything: Damien, my family, my work, Nina... I finally had my total power and control back.

## CHAPTER TWENTY-FOUR

The next day I phoned Nina. "Nina. I would like to see you. I had my session with Michael yesterday."

"And?"

"It went well."

"You are developing into a mature person, and I think a lot of the advice I have given you is falling on fruitful soil. I have not wasted my time. "

"But I want to talk to you about him. What is he really like?"

"I have told you many times that it is very important to understand your slave, that you have to listen, and that sometimes, the time you spend with your slave after the session is in fact the most important time. Sometimes this is more important than the session itself."

"You are right, Nina. I should have spent more time with him after the session. I dismissed him almost immediately."

"But you asked what Michael is really like. I

will tell you about the conversations Michael had with his psychologist. It will be very interesting for me to see what you think. Get ready and come over when you can Angelique."

I arrived at Nina's house an hour later.

Her husband Richard opened the door. He was a very good looking man, about fifteen years older than Nina. He was slim and immaculately dressed.

"Hello. You must be Angelique. My pleasure to meet you. Come let me take you to Nina. Can I get you a drink?"

"Thank you. Yes orange juice please," I replied a little taken back. I had never had a man wait on me before except in restaurants.

He showed me into to where Nina was sitting and then disappeared only to return with my orange juice and a serviette. I didn't see him again on that day.

"Your husband is so kind," I said, when Nina entered the room.

Nina frowned. "Yes he is, indeed. Now I thought you wanted to discuss Michael."

"You said he sees a psychologist."

"He does so then, let's discuss psychology. The Greeks call it the science of the soul. Do you really think anybody can look into your soul? Let alone analyse it?"

"I thought we would discuss Michael."

"But, like I said, Angelique, if you would listen: Michael is all about psychology.

"I have known Michael for well over five years - he is a simple man; he is an honest man. Michael had a large business and lost it all, because of some crazy financial advice from an 'expert.'

"After his divorce he tried very hard to understand himself, and spent many hours with a psychologist. What Michael told me made me furious and sad. He is like a parrot, repeating the words of his psychologist, probably whispered in his ear."

"Why? What did he say?"

"One day, when he talked to me about 'degradation' - a subject I did *not* bring up, but a subject he had discussed in therapy - he said he never felt degraded during or after a thrashing. Rather, he feels stronger, perhaps purified, or even reborn."

"I can understand this, Nina."

"Really? You can? He also told me that a whipping given before or after a public activity has a high dramatic value. The contrast between being dominated at one moment and being in complete command of a situation an hour later adds enormously to one's sense of achievement, and to the appreciation of the authority he wields. All these different elements enter into the situation at this moment, and he found it most difficult to attach appropriate weight to each."

"Wow, I think I could probably understand this."

"Yes, but Angelique, this was his psychologist speaking, not Michael necessarily. I've known him for five years, and yes, people really believe after a while that this is true and this is how they feel, because the psychologist told them so. Here is another story he told me:

"'An individual might be exposed to hunger or cold - they might be whipped, tortured, and frightened for days on end - as part of a ritual, from which the individual emerges reborn. This is largely lost in modern civilisation.'"

"Did you ask him who told him about these individuals?" I asked.

"I didn't even *have* to ask him: I knew. Do you know where these rituals are conducted? They are certainly *not* lost in modern civilisation. Every time Michael comes to me for a lashing, I listen - I let him talk. Sometimes, it takes a long time before they talk - I mean the slaves - but I am not judgmental, and I never ask why. One day he told me, very seriously:

"'Consider two men who voluntarily undergo an ordeal; one climbs a mountain, and when he reaches the summit, what greets him? Probably a blizzard, and then he has to climb down again. The other goes to a woman friend and submits to the ordeal of being whipped - if she is severe, she may be whipping past the point of acceptance. But when the ordeal is over, what does the man who has been whipped find? A lovely woman, possibly ready to make love to him.' Now, I ask you: which man has it better? Why should either of the men feel degraded?"

"Wow, Nina. What a thing to say."

"I know. The truth is Michael does not, nor does his psychologist, know why he likes this - he just does. Just like a rock climber doesn't know why he likes climbing rocks. But still, what a comparison: rock climbing and the whip."

## CHAPTER TWENTY-FIVE

I arrived at home well after midnight and found
a letter stuck to my door with tape:

"Dearest Angelique,

"I have just arrived home again from my
world travels, and feel that I want to see you at
once. I have not really lived, and I feel a little
tired, relaxed, but not at peace within myself.
You can give me all that I need. You are a
wonderful, glowing woman, rich in every way.
That is the female in all her wonder.

"You have a lovely, bounteous figure,
exquisite legs and feet (of which I am a
connoisseur), skin that would make the best silk
or satin seem coarse by comparison, and lips like
the petals of a rose, not to mention a few of your
minor attributes.

"The force of your personality, which comes
through your expression and gesture... well, this
is too much of a wonder and mystery to me as
yet to try to express in a letter. Perhaps one day,
the impressions of you, which have gone deep

into my unconscious beyond logic, will burst forth as a poem I will write down hurriedly, scarcely knowing what it means until I look at it afterwards - that might hint at what is in you.

"All my life, Angelique, I have had a desire to be the slave of a beautiful queen. Deep inside me, however odd it might seem to some people, this dream wanted to be real and whole.

"I didn't want to spoil it by putting a false goddess on the pedestal that (secretly) I knew was inferior to me in intelligence, taste, being and imagination.

"I tried with Nina - you know that! But I always felt degraded and soiled. Now, with you, I feel that I have met the real one. I can kneel to you with all of me, without any sense of falsehood.

"Please believe me (I say this in utter sincerity): I feel you are a real queen. Someone once said that great talent and great beauty are beyond all laws - they make their own. I feel this is so with you.

"Why should you bother with me?

"Ha, here is the fear. I am under no delusions about my attractions - I know I am a very attractive man. But all I have to offer you is a very sincere worship and submission. As I said, the pain in itself does not mean very much to me.

"If you had whipped me as you whip your hardest slaves, or even more, I would not have questioned your right to do so or ceased to adore you. I want to be your slave; in truth, to belong to you - to be owned by you. It is for you to decide what is best for me and how much or how little you want to use me.

"As far as I am concerned, I exist to be your slave, and that means you can do whatever you wish with me. As to your decision whether you want to give me life by making me your slave, that is for you to decide, my princess… my darling.

"The mirrored box I presented to you, and which I crafted myself, is a gift that is only suitable for a goddess. And you are one of those goddesses, not reported since classical times, which has come down to Earth. They were always noted for their kindness to the most unworthy males, who recognised their divinity.

"I adore you. I worship you. I love you.

"Geoffrey."

I had a couple of drinks and smoked.

This was the most incredible love letter I'd ever received. It was nice to be loved and adored, but it was too much.

I stood before the mirror in the bathroom, got undressed and looked at myself naked. I checked my body right, left and centre, in the large mirror on my bathroom door. Even without being dressed up, I could start to see that I was beautiful, although there were still many things which could be improved upon.

I took off my make-up, brushed my hair and tied it in a sticking-up ponytail.

I looked again. 'God, you are so average-looking, it is pathetic,' I thought. What on Earth were these guys talking about? If they saw me like this they would freak out. Why do they love and adore me? Is it just because I am their mistress? Can they love and adore me normally?

I went back into the living room and poured myself another gin and tonic.

I thought about Geoffrey. There were many things I admired: he was a successful businessman, he encouraged me to go to university, he liked to travel, investigated other cultures and understood these cultures. He had a European education, came from a good and educated family. And he was very attractive physically.

'I will sleep and call Nina tomorrow,' I thought.

I hardly slept at all.

The next day I rang Nina.

"Is Geoffrey giving you sleepless nights?"

"Yes, but how did you know?"

"I can *feel* you, Angelique."

"Oh Nina, if only you could feel me as I feel you. But really, this letter from Geoffrey is too much. You should read the letter he wrote - page after page adoring me. It's driving me nuts, and I'm starting to worry that I can't handle these slaves - they really are too much for me."

"What you need to do is get a driving licence."

"What, Nina? I'm talking about Geoffrey."

"I know. But really, this is much more important - you need a driving licence. You have been in this country for over six months now. So you need to take a test."

"Okay."

"Now, let me explain something about Geoffrey - I know you find him super-attractive, but I told you once and I'll tell you again: no love affair with Geoffrey; no sex with Geoffrey. You give him a session, just like you did with Michael - you spend two and a half hours with him, and that is it.

"Let him take you to the theatre, or the opera, or the ballet - all the stuff you like to do;

he will take you. Parade around with him - all the girls will envy you. Let him take you out for dinner after or before university. Just never hop into bed with him - you can never, ever have sex with a slave. Is that okay?"

I didn't understand, but I knew Nina was right: Nina was always right.

## CHAPTER TWENTY-SIX

I arranged to meet Geoffrey outside my
apartment that weekend. When I saw him with
his light blue suit, vest and light pink shirt, my
heart began thumping and I could not stop
looking at him. He looked like a model.

When he saw me he ran and gave me a big
hug, and kissed me lightly on the cheek. He
took my hands and showered them with kisses.

When we got into the car, he brought up the
fact that he had not had a single session with me,
other than the one with Nina.

"I loved your gentle caresses when you ran
your hands over my body, while I was helpless
in your chains at Nina's place. Your movements
are beautiful and sensuous, and you dance
beautifully. Sometimes I would like to be
danced, with you leading - I would adore feeling
the movement of your lovely body lead and
direct mine."

"I did dance with you, Geoffrey. Remember
the party? We danced at least ten times that

night."

"You are right. When you finally danced with me I asked you to lead, and then I saw another aspect of you: you seemed such a fierce little soul, determined to carry off this leading bit, so gallant and courageous in your confrontation of life. I felt in myself a sort of fierce protectiveness towards you."

I laughed.

"You won't see this manifest unless it ever does become necessary to protect you, but if it ever does, then you will see such a resolve and fierceness that it will shake anyone who tries to hurt you. Many women would not believe this, thinking that a man who would be their slave and servant must be always weak. But you, I believe, know people and realise that it is not as simple as that."

"You are not my slave, Geoffrey, and that night at Nina's was a long ago."

He stopped the car at the red light, and he quickly put it into park.

He leant over to me, took my face and kissed me.

I was very tempted to kiss him back, but I was glad when the light changed to green and he had to keep on driving.

"Another thing I disagree with you on,

Angelique, is that you can never come to really know me when you give me only a fraction of yourself. I don't believe any woman will ever come to know me! She'd have to give all of herself - total commitment - before I could give her all of myself."

"Total commitment? Oh my!" 'Total commitment - not for me right now,' I thought.

"It's not that I wouldn't go for a one-sided situation myself, it's just that the essential law of human relations won't allow anything else, and though you think I have a sense of inferiority, it's not: it's a sense of hopelessness in trying to deal with the shallowness of the world. I doubt you will ever meet another man whom it would be more worthwhile to know."

"I think you are a wonderful and interesting man," I said, "but presently I am just not in a position to commit myself to anybody."

"I realise this, because it would be the emotional equivalent of jumping off a precipice in the dark - not knowing if it was two feet down or a thousand. Having said this, I hope you are not annoyed. I have been completely honest, because I love you, even though it may lose me what I have. Now, if you allow it, I will step back into my role as one of the minor characters in your play."

"You are not a minor character in my play, Geoffrey. In fact, you are the only man I am going out with presently. We have spent an awful lot of time together, and every time I am with you, I am happy and content. So, why not leave it just like that? We are wonderful friends, and we have great conversations – I'd like to keep it that way!"

He parked the car in the parking lot across from the King Edward Hotel, in downtown Toronto. He picked me up and carried me across the street to the entrance of the hotel.

"Honeymooners, come on in!" laughed the doorman.

"I wish, I wish!" replied Geoffrey, and we walked into the dining room.

It was one of the finest places one could dine in Toronto. Classical music played while waiters hovered around. The silverware sparkled, and the dishes were light porcelain. The whole place was first class, and I felt like a princess. It was a place I could never afford to visit on my own.

Geoffrey selected a private table at the window and ordered Champagne cocktails - my favourite drinks.

Then he looked at me and folded his hands, and I noticed the perfectly manicured fingernails, and the diamond rings on his little fingers. His pitch-black eyes and the shining black hair surrounded his fine, chiselled face and light-brown skin. I could not stop looking at him, and for a moment I imagined him in bed with me. I thought it would be glorious to have this man.

I thought about why I liked Geoffrey so much: it was because he put me on a pedestal - he admired me. He wanted to read the books I've read, and he wanted to hear the music I've liked. He was interested in opera, ballet, theatre, and philosophy. I told him about Tantra yoga. Despite the fact that I was so young and he was considerably older than I was, he treated me like a grown-up, successful female. I felt equal to him, not like with Damien, who treated me like I was a young dumb girl, soon to be a young dumb housewife.

Then I remembered that Nina had told me never to have sex with a slave.

"You never told me what you thought about my letter," he said, gently and sadly. "It took me hours and hours to write - I must have spent a whole afternoon. I really tried to express my feelings, and yet you never mentioned a word."

"Oh, I am sorry Geoffrey! It was one of the nicest letters I have ever received. I've read it

171

many times, but I never see myself the way you
described me - perhaps that was the reason
I never mentioned it. Geoffrey, I would love to
know a bit about your family and how you grew
up."

"I was born with a silver spoon in my
mouth, I guess, right? Spoiled - the only child - I
received everything could do... anything I liked.
I attended the best schools - boarding schools in
Switzerland, etc. My father was an admiral, and
my mother never worked. I was her life.

"When I was a little boy, I always wanted to
run and tell my mother anything that had
happened or show her anything I had done. Not
to boast - I just wanted to say: 'This is for you.
because I love you!'"

"But this is lovely, Geoffrey. What was your
mother like?"

"You are as beautiful as she was, just in
another way. You are full of this wonderful
warmth, tenderness, kindness and compassion:
the essence of womanhood - it is cherishing,
loving, and understanding beyond all reason.
The man who ever gets this will be very, very
lucky."

I smiled and thought: 'Oh, how gorgeous
you are.'

"Now I understand your defences, because

you have this pearl and you hesitate to cast it before swine. Yes, I am tall, dark, slim, rich, clever and charming," he laughed, and smoked a cigarette, leaning back in his chair. He smiled, rolled his eyes, and continued gently: "But I have lived long enough to know that even as I am all of those things, I would probably understand nothing of you. As it is, I have experienced you many times - your kindness, compassion, tenderness... and I will never forget it."

"How can you say that I hesitate to cast my pearl before swine? You are indeed tall, dark, rich, clever and charming - you forgot beautiful, too. So what do you want?"

"I wish we could make love, Angelique. For one thing, this is a way in which much of what is in me could be transferred to you. The act of love is much more than physical. I love you, and it would be a very wonderful experience for me to be taken into your very self, my darling - my queen."

'Oh, my God,' I thought, 'if I was alone with him in my apartment, I think I would melt.'

"I know I am not worthy, but who is worthy of anything? Naturally, I see myself as totally submissive to you, with you riding triumphantly upon me. Or perhaps as your slave in the

173

dominant position. May I fantasise? I wish you to humble me, and I will tell you the best way to do it."

'Please, Geoffrey,' I thought; 'please do not start talking this way.'

"Put straps around my ankles, connected by a very short chain, so that I have to take dainty little steps. Then put a leather collar and chain round my neck. Wear your dark net stockings and those pretty shoes of yours, with the little strap across the instep. Then command me: 'Kiss my boots, slave!' and give me a sharp blow with your riding crop from time to time. While I am doing this, say: 'Kiss harder, slave!'"

In an instant, my admiration and high opinion of him were gone.

I remembered the night when he stood in front of Nina's window, looking out into the garden. Nina had slapped his face and told him to kiss her boots, and he had knelt down and kissed her boots while she hit him with a whip again and again - he had said nothing.

By the expression on my face, he must have noticed that something he said had made me feel terrible - something had gone awfully wrong.

"You are snow white and perspiring, Angelique!" he said. He got up and sat beside me. He took my face in his hands again, cupping it tenderly, and kissed me.

It was a wonderful kiss, and I returned it. Then I pushed him away.

He got up and sat across me again.

"I must be honest here," he whispered with tears in his eyes; "I must be honest and say what I feel very deeply. It is difficult, so please don't be angry with me if I stumble or fail to communicate clearly what I mean. I am trying hard out of love for you to be honest, and it is not easy. So please be kind and understanding, my Madonna - my love, my queen."

"Please excuse me, Geoffrey," I said, "I need to go to the powder room."

I thought I was going to vomit. I think I had too much to drink.

I looked into the mirror. 'Geez, you are sweating.' I took out my make-up kit and started to fix my face. I sprayed myself with perfume. 'Breathe deep,' I thought; 'breathe - take in that air, and breathe out that air. Breathe... breathe...'

I returned to the dining room.

"Oh, Angelique," he said. He looked at me, astonished. He reached over the table, took my hands, and pressed them hard. He said,

"You will never, ever be second in line with me, Angelique. I want to help you to develop and to become more of yourself, right through

175

your life to the end."

'Oh, Geoffrey,' I thought, 'how wonderful to hear you say this!' But I said nothing - just looked at him.

"I want to help you to express yourself fully in life, as a writer, or an actress with an audience, or as an executive with many employees. I love you, and I want you to become yourself, fully."

"Do you really?" I asked.

"I am a big enough man, and I have got beyond the stage of trying to keep women down, for fear that they might prove better than I am."

"I know that, and this is why I like you so much."

"I want you to express yourself in a way you feel is needed for you. I respect you as another human-being. I hope you can reciprocate, and you can understand that I am not less a man because of this, but *more* of a man. If you ever come to respect my innermost spirit and cherish it with your woman's love, then the rest of the world can go away - I will be yours forever."

The waiter brought the food, and we ate.

We ate without talking.

I listened to the music and thought: 'I wonder if Geoffrey were not a slave, he would be the man of my dreams. How can I deal with this slave business? Will he ever let me know why he needs to be whipped and flogged?

'How can I make love to him when he insists that it be in chains? I think the world of him, but I do not understand this craving. Why does he want a leather collar and chain around his neck?'

I had not said anything, but Geoffrey spoke at once, answering my thoughts:

"I need the fantasy; I need the suspense; I need the demonstrative feature, Angelique."

I just looked at him and nodded.

He continued: "I may admit defeat, but I realise that I am undefeatable. My complete surrender is nothing but an intensification of a scornful rebellion - my obedience will kill your commands; my acceptance will make you powerless. The acknowledgement of your power is my preparation for your overthrow. If you beat, tie and humiliate me, I will attain my pleasure. I will bear everything, but I will never renounce my satisfaction.

"By fully submitting, I remain totally independent, and I will never yield. Since I ordered my own punishment, I am the master of my own destiny..."

"Geoffrey... I-"

"Angelique, all I want to know is will you grant me a session?"

I nodded: "Yes, Geoffrey, I will."

## CHAPTER TWENTY-SEVEN

In between Michael, Geoffrey and Nina, I had also been seeing my other slaves, including Rod Keith and Peter. My schedule was serving its purpose and working very well. I would see one slave every evening, Monday to Thursday, then two slaves on a Friday and Saturday.

The only exception would be that every fortnight I would take Saturday off and stay with Nina at her cottage.

Most sessions lasted between two and three hours, including time that I would spend with the slave before, or more importantly, after.

The good thing was that most of the slaves Nina sent me, she already knew. There were a few occasions when there would be a new slave, that Nina had not been mistress over before - on these occasions she and her husband would vet them extensively, before passing them to me.

I was with Nina at her cottage when she told me about a new slave, who wanted to have a session with me:

"His name is Stephen and he is American. I was going to vet him, but he said he knows you."

The memories of being left in Paris by my so-called friend - my American pen-pal - came flooding back to me. I shuddered as I remembered how alone I felt.

Nina put her arm round me. "I can tell him you said no, if you wish."

"No. I mean… I don't know. How did he find me?"

"Angelique, he did not find you. It is by coincidence or by choice of the Fates. You know, in ancient Greece the Fates, or Moriah, were female-like representations of destiny – they chose the path of the humans. It appears that they have guided him to you."

I took a breath. I was nervous and upset about seeing Stephen. But then I thought: 'I am not that same naive little girl any more. I have nothing to be ashamed of - it is he who was in the wrong; it was he who was married with children, lying about his age to seduce a young girl.'

"I will meet him," I said to Nina. "But tell him he must take me out first, before I agree to a session."

"Angelique, you can't fuck a slave, even

before you agree to a session with them. It's very dangerous."

"I know. I have no intention of doing either."

When I arrived back from the cottage that Sunday night, Nina had left a message saying that she had spoken to Stephen and he had agreed to take me out in two days' time. I would spend until then getting ready for him.

On the day I was meant to meet Stephen, I spent two hours with my hairdresser. The hairdresser not only created a spectacular hairdo, but I paid for a special make-up artist to attend to me.

I knew I looked fantastic.

I wore an outfit that Nina had chosen: a black lace dress, with my black silk stiletto heels and my black pearl purse. Nina gave me a black mink coat.

Through Nina, I arranged to meet Stephen outside his hotel, but I told him he must pay for the car.

When I arrived at his shoddy hotel, I got out of the chauffeur-driven car and waited for him. I knew immediately where I wanted him to take me - somewhere fancy and expensive.

He gawked when he stepped out of the hotel and saw me.

"Hello Stephen," I said.

"My God, Angelique, you are more beautiful than I ever imagined or dreamt."

He leant forward and kissed me on the cheek.

I looked at him. He was recognisable from the pictures he had sent me, but only by the face. He had evidently once been quite handsome, when he had the pictures taken, but now he had let himself go: he had s large belly, a double-chin and bags under his eyes.

"Let's go to the King Edward Hotel for dinner," I said.

His face dropped. I knew he was intimidated. I was happy: he deserved it.

"I already have a reservation booked somewhere else," he said.

"Stephen , you don't know Canada that well, but there is nowhere else which is as nice as the King Edward, and this is a special occasion."

He forced a smile.

"I have thought many years about seeing you," I said and leant over to kiss him.

He smiled again and got into the car.

When we arrived at the King Edward and entered the elegant dining room, all the waiters said hello to me by name and made a real fuss over me. The attention I was received blew

Stephen away.

"You seem to be doing very well for yourself, the gorgeous Angelique," he said.

I smiled.

When the waiter came I ordered lobster, Champagne and the most expensive dinner I could.

Stephen couldn't stop flinching.

Throughout the meal Stephen just kept staring at me, and he had very little to say.

After dinner I got up before even waiting for desert.

"Thank you for a great night, Stephen. But I must go now - I have other people to see."

He looked up at me in total disbelief. His mouth was open - he was speechless.

"Have a safe journey back to Buffalo, and thank you for buying me dinner. Send my regards to your wife and children."

His mouth stayed open but he didn't respond.

I strode out of the dining room, and never even turned around.

## CHAPTER TWENTY-EIGHT

I had taken Nina's advice and booked a driving test. Nina insisted on coming with me.

When she arrived she was unusually wearing make-up, and looked even more stunning then she did normally - she looked like a model from *Vogue*.

She told the driving examiner that she was my sister and that she just wanted to sit in the back of the car. She flirted with the driving instructor as if he was God's gift to the world. During the test she kept talking about how wonderfully I was doing - she never once stopped.

I passed my test and I had my driver's license.

"All I was waiting for was for you to put your hand in his pants," I said.

"I would have done that, too!" she laughed.

Nothing in my life was more enjoyable than driving Nina up to her cottage. I could look forward to two days of total harmony and peace.

We were alone, and we could talk. She never listened to music in the car - she just listened to me.

"Today, you are my private chauffeur," said Nina.

"I would love to drive you around the world! Tell me, Nina: what do you personally feel after a session with a slave? How does it affect you?"

"I feel hot as hell in the my outfit! But I think how hard it was to work in the factory, and how easy this kind of work is."

"No, but how do you feel about these men? They must be under an awful lot of pressure in their lives that they need this to relax."

"They go home happy. They forget the lousy world for a while, and they always appreciate me, because they always come back to me."

"Nina, sometimes I feel embarrassed about the money. It seems to me that what they leave is so much, and I wonder if my sessions are worth that type of money. I often feel ashamed when I notice what two hours of that stuff has cost them. And sometimes I do nothing, absolutely nothing at all, and they left me an amazing amount of cash."

"Angelique, I have told you before that I do not like speaking about money. But, who are you to argue with the price they feel your time is worth, and with their generosity? If they were dissatisfied with your services, they would not call you for another appointment, would they? You are human - you have to live. I have never told anybody how much a session would be, but surprisingly I have never been disappointed. If they cannot afford it, they would not return. *They* set the price - *you* didn't."

We had arrived at her cottage and wandered down the hill. It was dark by now, but the full moon illuminated the area. It was very quiet and peaceful.

"We'll make a fire down by the lake," she said. "Let's go for a swim, and then we eat."

The cottage door was open. Everything looked as immaculate as we had left it. There were two deck-chairs positioned around the open fire.

"Don't you ever lock the door?" I said.

She said nothing, undressed, handed me a robe, took her familiar picnic basket and we went down to the beach.

It was fantastic to swim naked at night. We swam out to a small island made in the middle of the lake.

"You are a good swimmer. Are you still okay?"

I nodded, and we sat next to each other on the stones of a little island. She picked up a frog.

It sat on her hand, and she stroked its body carefully with one finger. Then she took my hand, put the frog on it, and smiled. "It will take a good half hour to swim back - it will keep you in shape. Are you cold?"

Without waiting for an answer, she slid back into the water and swam back.

I put the frog down and followed after her.

Back on the beach, we sat in our robes in the lounge chairs, watching the flickering fire. It felt as if though we were the only two people in the world. I watched the shimmering stars, way up in the beautiful, dark blue sky.

"Do you know anything about the stars?" I asked. "Do you know their names?"

"No, but I wish I could."

"Tell me about your childhood, Nina. How did you grow up?"

"Why would you want to know about that?"

"Because it is you, Nina. I want to know you, but I don't want to hurt you."

"Nobody has ever asked me that question."

"Not even your husband?"

"*Especially* not Richard - he knows it only brings up bad memories. You see, my darling, I didn't grow up privileged like you did: my entire childhood was a horrible disaster. One should forget the past, and live for now and the future. Therefore, I don't talk about my childhood."

"Tell me something nice - something that made you very happy. Do you remember something like that?"

"There is one story that I treasure: I was about seventeen, so it was 1941. We lived in a relatively good neighbourhood in Moscow. Half of it was bombed out, but behind our row house, protected by a huge, six-foot wall, was an embassy. You were not even born then, but waiting for the stork to pick you."

"Was this the time when Hitler bombed the city?"

"Yes, you cannot imagine the devastation. You thought you were poverty-stricken in Paris, but you have no idea what poverty really means - we had nothing. When the weather was fine, we used to sit on that high stone wall. We climbed up on a ladder, and it was the boundary between our small backyard and a beautiful, old fairyland-like park. We could look into that park, but we could never walk into it because it belonged to and was protected by the staff of the embassy."

"And what did you see?"

"We watched the embassy employees often, under many tree branches, and protected from their eyes. I would even sit there with my girlfriends - the girls I worked with in the laundry shop. We were totally covered by leaves, and we noticed females arrive in the garden in the late afternoon - they were dressed in long trailing gowns, dresses our mothers never used to wear."

"In 1941, in the middle of the war, they had evening gowns?"

"Yes, that was the magic. These embassy people were super-rich, we thought. First, the ladies walked around silently, but the more they drank from the beer bottles, the louder they got. Sometimes there was music, but usually very late and when it was almost dark. We loved to listen to that music."

"Live music, like an orchestra?"

"Real live music! We saw the men with black suits and jackets, with long black tails, like birds. Each of them had a woman pressed tightly against them, and they would be walking and turning, all in the same area. They looked funny to us, but very nice too."

"They wore suits like a conductor, when I listened to the symphony orchestra in France."

"Yes, it is called a swallowtail coat, or a

189

tailcoat. You can't imagine how impressive the whole scene looked. We never saw movies - there was no television - and certainly no live music. I can't remember ever dancing with anybody anywhere."

"I love you so much, Nina. Tell me, why are you my friend? Why are you doing all these things for me?"

"Because I can see that it's worth my while, and it truly makes me happy - I have not been as happy for a very long time. There are alot of things you will have to learn, but all these experiences will make you strong - very strong - and you will never have to eat peanuts and worry that you'll end up hungry, like in Paris."

"Would you have loved to have children, Nina?"

"Yes, but I never got pregnant, thank God."

"But if you had?"

"If I had a daughter like you, then yes - you are the sunshine of my life."

"What do you think is the most important thing I have to learn right now?"

"You have to learn the difference between infatuation and love."

"I don't know the difference."

"Infatuation could be a passionate absorption in the moment, a sexual foolishness,

or a momentary and senseless love. It is natural
for all of your slaves to be infatuated with you as
their mistress, but do not mistake this for
anything like love. For you, you are presently
infatuated with Geoffrey just because you find
him attractive and interesting, but you don't love
him. You have loved only one man in your life:
Damien."

"But Geoffrey loves me! You've read his
letter - have you ever seen a letter like that? You
didn't hear what he said to me: he wants to put
me on a pedestal."

"To receive a letter like that for the first time
is... well, I would say it's almost intimidating.
But when you've been in this business for a
while, you will receive many letters just like
Geoffrey's. It is typical for a masochist to write a
letter just like that."

"But I know Geoffrey loves me: he spelled it
out with every word."

Nina rolled her eyes; "Well, if Geoffrey said
it, it must be true. You have to be careful,
Angelique: you have no idea what men are
capable of when they are in love, my darling.
Not only that, but if you have sex with a slave
then it can be very bad: it crosses the line into
what some would say is prostitution. If one man
were to become angry and report you, you

would have great trouble."

"I know you care about me, Nina, but Geoffrey would never hurt me and I will do a session with him."

"No. I will do the session with you and Geoffrey - you will not do it alone. We will give him a session he will never forget."

"Thank you, Nina." I leant over and kissed her.

It was past midnight.

"Would you like a drink? Or perhaps a cigarette?"

I shook my head. I felt tired.

"Would you like to sleep?"

I nodded.

She took my hand, and she kissed me on the cheek and wished me goodnight.

I looked at her face next to me in bed, the moon illuminating her hair. She is the most beautiful woman I have ever seen.

## CHAPTER TWENTY-NINE

Nina and I prepared everything in my apartment. All the light-bulbs had been switched to red, the hanging flower-pots had been removed from the steel bar, the whips were laid out and the slave robe was placed on the small chair in the entrance.

All ready for Geoffrey.

Geoffrey, as expected, arrived exactly on time. Down to the minute.

When I heard the knock on the door, I asked him to come in. He could not see me, because the entrance hall and the living room were divided, and shielded by the heavy black velvet curtain.

I heard him close the door softly.

"Put on the slave robe I've laid out for you, and when you are ready, sit down with your back to the curtain, and touch the bells so I know that you are done," I instructed him.

"Yes Angelique, Princess, I will."

"No more speaking, Geoffrey."

193

I sat and waited.

I'm sure he was purposely getting dressed slowly, to annoy me.

"I am ready, Mistress," he declared.

I gritted my teeth - I had told him to ring the bells and not to speak. As usual, he could not do what he was told.

I decided not to reply and just wait.

Finally, he rang the bells.

I walked behind him and handcuffed his wrists behind his back. Then I blindfolded him twice, so I knew that that there was no way he could see anything.

"I'm all mixed up about you: in some ways, I think I know everything, and in other ways, I feel like a complete idiot - a mongoloid idiot. In one part of my mind, I feel that I am the only man in this wide world who can awaken you to what you really are, and yet, at the same time, I feel like a garbage man, looking at a countess stepping out of a Rolls Royce."

"I don't need a Rolls Royce, Geoffrey, and you are not a mongoloid idiot. I am wide awake - you don't have to awaken me. And you need to stop talking."

"Anyone can dream, but what about hope? All I know is that there is a big, empty space inside me that has 'Angelique' written across it.

You must take over from here, because I have reached the limit of what I can understand or bear in my emotions or thoughts. You must know, because, in the end, knowing is the woman's job, as is mercy and the giving of life at all levels."

2I am in charge now Geoffrey," I said, "so get up and I will take care of the rest."

He easily stood, even whilst restrained.

"It is such a relief to hear you say: 'let me take care of the rest'," he said; "this is what I really want. I want to be your slave, your property, your instrument - not to make decisions, but to carry out yours."

I did not reply, but looked and admired his body.

His legs were really toned and muscular - I could see just to the top of his thighs. I wondered how big his penis was.

His torso looked even more muscular and tanned then when I had seen it last time. He had a broad, toned chest, big, round shoulders, and I could see the lines of his stomach muscles.

Even his after-shave made me want him. I wanted to touch myself almost as much as I wanted to touch him.

I led him into the living room, stepped on a stool, unlocked the cuffs quickly, and chained his wrists to the bar.

For a few seconds, he was totally free, but he stretched out his second arm while I chained the first, and it was obvious that he did not want to escape.

Then I did what I had wanted to do for a long time: I touched him.

I ran my hands over his back, his shoulders and down his arms, as I stood over him, and chained his hands above him.

I knelt down and lifted up his slave cloth, slipped my hands under the band of his boxer shorts and felt his growing penis in my hand. I slowly pulled down his underwear - when they reached the floor he stepped out of them.

Then, I fastened his ankles. I took the opportunity to run my hand up and down the back of his legs. I stroked his bum, his thighs and his calves.

The touch of his bare skin made me quiver with excitement. My pussy was so wet. He was so gorgeous. I wanted him so badly.

I stood up and put my arms around his neck and kissed him.

His huge erection pressed against me as my tongue entered his mouth. It was a wonderful kiss, full of passion.

My hands went under his robe and grabbed

his bum. It felt like pure muscle. I squeezed it hard, as I continued to kiss him.

I brought my hand round to the front of his body and grabbed his hard penis. I masturbated it with my hand.

Geoffrey moaned.

He was so hard - so erect.

I spread my legs and put his penis against my pussy. I looked at him. He was blindfolded and could not see me.

"Do you really want the punishment now, Geoffrey, or do you want to make love to me."

He bent his head forward, kissed my shoulder and said: "I admire your air of authority very much - the way you left me sitting, awaiting your pleasure, before you chained me up. You have such an air of authority when you adjust the chains.

"When you do whip me, I know you judge carefully where to hit, and watch the expression on my face, studying my reactions. You are so clever, and you know the sensitive spots so that I cannot hide them. I may wince, and I suppose my face will show that I experience pain."

My heart sank.

I felt a burst of anger. "Well, Geoffrey, if pain is what you want, then pain is what you will get."

I looked at Nina and nodded.

Nina stepped forward with the bull-whip.

"I hope you will remove the blindfolds," he said. "I hope you will tempt and tease me with your lovely body, as you dance in triumph before your helpless slave."

"She will not be doing anything," sneered Nina, as she stepped forward and brought the bull-whip crashing down on his back.

*Whack.*

"Arghh," Geoffrey groaned in pain.

I walked into the bathroom, closed the door and sat down.

That groan was the last sound I heard from Geoffrey all night, despite me listening to the crack of the whip for over an hour.

Nina came into bathroom when it was all done and closed the door.

"I'm done. He is tough - very tough. Apart from that first noise he made, which I think was more out of surprise, he did not mumble, he did not moan, wince or stagger. And I really beat him - I beat him *hard*. If I didn't stop, I'm sure I would have killed him."

"Did he not say anything?"

"Not a word, my angel - not even an expression on his face. He stood there, stone-faced, and with a slight grin around his mouth until the end. He did not even move his body. He is the most disciplined slave you can imagine. I hope you are as disciplined, Angelique, and I hope you are not crawling into bed with him. Believe me, he cannot perform tonight - he needs some rest."

Then Nina left.

I stayed in the bathroom and smoked.

I did not want to see him, afraid of the damage I would see.

When I finally did go to him, I was shocked.

His buttocks and back were covered in blood. His body was plastered with welts, so neatly placed, one after the other, and precisely, as if they had been painted with a fine, red paintbrush. His arms and legs were black and swollen.

I couldn't believe it.

I took off the blindfold, and he looked at me with tears in his eyes.

"Geoffrey, why are you doing this?" I cried out. I stepped onto the stool and took the chains off his wrists. "Please. This is terrible! Why do you insist on doing this?"

Geoffrey just looked through me and said: "I think I have finally absorbed the lesson you wanted to teach me. I now realise at a more deep level that I am your slave, that it isn't always easy, but that it is a fate I'm not going to escape from, and it's not a game. You can really do with me what you wish. I said before that I wanted to be owned by you, but I realise now that I didn't fully realise what I was saying. I have suddenly become aware that I am totally owned by you."

"Let me cream your back!" I cried. "Please sit down on this stool and let me put some soothing lotion on you. Even better, lie down on your stomach, so I can cream everything to make you feel better."

He stood there, not moving as I held his hands in front of me.

"I realise that you are way ahead of me and that your plan for me will unfold in its own good time, at the pace you choose, and that my destiny is in your hands. I wish that you would come to feel some need or affection for me. I would not wish that you felt the need that I feel, because I love you, and I would not wish such a torturing need on anyone, let alone someone I love."

"Oh, Geoffrey!" I cried. "This is not me - really it is not! It is not good for me, it is not good for you, so please, let me take care of you."

He smiled and gave me a big hug. His entire body was shaking.

"You must derive a good deal of amusement, my princess, from observing my absurd attempts at self-importance. For I think you know already that you are going to subjugate me to the point where I am merely the instrument of your will."

"This is not my will, Geoffrey!" I shouted; "This is *your* will - your insane wish to be punished. And for what?"

"When you were putting the chains around my wrists," he said, very seriously, "I had the sense of an inexorable plan you had for me, which would move on to its end, despite anything I might think, or say, or wish - that my life had been taken over. There is the prospect of much suffering in this for me, for I ache with anguish for your presence, but I have no choice but to submit to your will."

Then he walked into the hallway and got dressed. Very slowly, he put on one piece after the other and said: "I realise that though you are someone of great importance in my life, I am only one of many in yours. You have so many to look after, and I believed you when you said you take care of all your slaves. You sounded so very warm and loving to them all. So keep me in line, Angelique, and don't let me be bothersome."

He reached into his suit jacket and took out an envelope. He put in onto the chair, looked at me, touched my hair, and opened the door. Then he took my face and kissed me lightly on the forehead.

"I will call you when I am back in Canada," he said. "I will always love you. In your case, you have already given to me very generously, so there is no worry about that. The fact that I genuinely love you is not surprising. Though this is the first time, it has been personal sexual love as well, for me."

He closed the door.

When I opened the envelope I realised that there was more money in it than I had ever received. I looked for a note - there was none, just a lot of money. I wanted a note: a love letter - anything but money.

I sat in my living room and looked at the bar, the chains and the whips. I drank gin and tonic, smoked cigarettes and cried.

## CHAPTER THIRTY

It had been six days since our session with
Geoffrey and I had stayed in bed for all of them.

I had taken my phone off the hook and had
not met or spoke to any of my normal slaves. I
just couldn't face them.

I had not even spoken to Nina. I was so
lonely - I hadn't felt this way since the bad times
in Paris.

I willed myself to get up off the sofa. I
decided to check the answer-phone. When I
switched it on, it was filled with messages. Peter,
one of my other slaves, had announced he would
be in Toronto on Friday night and that he would
like a session. Two other slaves - Kenneth and
Keith - had also left messages. Michael had left a
message asking about our session later tonight,
but I had completely forgotten about that, and
was in no mood to meet with him.

But there was none from Nina, although she
never would leave a message, and always
expected me to answer.

I desperately needed to speak to Nina. I plugged my phone in and called her.

No answer.

I rang Nina again at five in the afternoon. Still no answer.

My heart started to thump.

I ran into the garage, jumped into my car, and drove to her house.

The house was in darkness.

I opened up the gate and walked around the house. 'Her dog, Max, must be here,' I thought, but the dog-house was empty. The garage doors were locked, and so were the front door and all the side doors.

I felt like I had been hit by an avalanche.

Why would she leave and not call? Maybe she's gone: the world trip! She's taken the cruise.

I was filled with fear and pain. I went back to my car.

I decided to drive up to the cottage to see if Nina had retreated to there.

When I got there, the cottage, too, was in darkness, with all the windows and even the door locked. This was particularly strange as Nina never locked the door.

I sat in my car, just staring out the window. I didn't know what to do... what to think. I felt so alone - so lost.

I sat and thought. The only person I could think of now was Lisa. But I didn't even know her last name, so I could not look her up in the telephone book. I began to shake. I knew where Lisa lived, so I decided to drive to her house.

When I got there, I was initially elated when I saw several cars parked outside, but then I realised none of them were Nina's.

I sat across the street, in my car, and started to cry.

I looked at Lisa's house again and waited. I was afraid to knock on her door, so I wrote down my phone number and posted it through her door.

Then I came home and called Nina again, but again there was no answer.

I waited by the phone for another hour.

Then it rang.

"Nina!?" I shrieked down the phone.

"No, it's Lisa."

"Lisa! God! Have you heard from Nina? Do you know if she is okay?"

"She is okay. She is in Calgary."

"In Calgary? Why is she on the other side of Canada? What she doing there? How I can reach her?"

"You can't reach her. Richard's brother had an accident - a car accident - so they both took off immediately."

"Oh, okay. Why didn't she tell me?"

Lisa paused before answering: "Maybe she didn't have time because it was an emergency."

"If you speak to her can you tell her to call me urgently please?"

"Of course - no problem. Are you okay, Angelique?"

"Yeah, I am fine," I lied, and then I hung up.

Then I cried some more.

## CHAPTER THIRTY-ONE

I was lying on my sofa, drinking gin, when I heard a knock on my door.

My heart jumped at the thought of Nina; even if she hadn't received my message from Lisa, she would have sensed that I was in pain and come to me.

When I opened the door, I was disappointed to see Michael standing there holding a record under his arm.

"I'm sorry Angelique; I tried to call you to confirm our session. But I had not heard from you, and could not get an answer from the phone. Are you okay?"

I looked at Michael and burst into tears.

As much as I did not want to see him, it was good to have someone there to talk to.

Michael immediately stepped forward to hug me. It was the first time we'd had physical contact.

I invited Michael in. We drank, and I told him about Geoffrey, and that I felt like a wounded animal.

"I have been where you are, Angelique - my whole life was broken up."

He smiled. It reminded me of when my father used to smile.

"When a person reaches the point of this awakening, there must always be one who is already awakened with him or her, and one will always come. A person could be in the Arctic or the jungle, and there would always be one of us there at the right time. We do nothing: we are just a channel - maybe we talk and answer questions if the person wishes, but we are not in control or forcing anything."

"Are you talking about faith, Michael?" I asked.

"It may not necessarily be religion; the person's own higher self is the one which awakens them, when it knows that at last they are ready. Always, the person has to help in some way, without knowing that this is a condition. Sometimes we are put in a position where we are - for instance: destitute - just to give the person a chance. It happened to me once - I don't think it will happen again. It was a test of me too - a novice on his first case - to see if I would really do anything."

"I know how your wife took your every

penny and left you for broke - that is tragic," I replied.

"Geoffrey is also tragic. Tragic is the gateway to wisdom. I know that our age does not care for the tragic - that is because it is a bourgeois age: an interregnum between the deaths of one civilisation and the rise of another. There is nothing I could do to make this happen, and there is nothing I could teach you: these things can only be experienced by oneself," Michael replied.

"Nina explained to me the difference between love and infatuation," I said.

"And how do you feel about me? Am I just your slave? I wish to be as that which you will Geoffrey to be."

"Wait here," I said: "I'll be back with you in a moment."

I went into the bathroom to splash water in my face. I felt terrible - completely shattered.

I went to the kitchen, made us both a drink and returned to the living room. Michael was sitting on the floor and I sat down on the sofa.

"I'm sorry I said that, Angelique," he said, turning round. "I have destroyed everything! I shouldn't have said that. You are like a beautiful dream. Please, Angelique, listen to my record. I would so very much like to play it for you. It is exotic dream music - I would like your dream to return right now."

Michael reached up and gave me the record he had been holding. It was the album of Nino Rote's music from the film *"Juliet of the Spirits"* - one of my very favourite films.

I got up and went to play it. When I returned I bent down, took Michael's hands in mine and lifted him to me. His large hands made mine look like tiny, captured birds.

"I don't just want to be your slave, Angelique. I did not craft this apartment just to your slave: I did it so that you would love me."

I stroked his hair, not knowing whether I felt love, sympathy for him or pity for myself.

I pressed my face against his and hugged him. His arms cuddled me back.

"I do love you, Michael!" I said. "I love you so very much right now."

His tears rubbed off on my cheeks.

'Love… perhaps this is the love that I could not have with Damien, and the love I will never find with Geoffrey or Nina. Perhaps this is it. Oh, love,' I thought; 'finally I have found you again.'

We played the record he had brought me over and over again.

Michael was close to me.

His body was close to me.

He kissed my hands and my arms, my neck and my cheeks.

I wondered what I could possibly feel for him. Was it that I was lonesome? Was it that I pitied him? Or myself?

It couldn't have been his looks. But why shouldn't I just enjoy the moment, and this delicious feeling, as long as it lasts?

Michael looked at his watch and showed it to me: it was past midnight. He got up to go.

The thought of his leaving terrified me.

I wanted to possess him. I wanted nothing more than to make love to him and have him with me hour after hour. I realised that the next morning I would probably feel terrible - I knew so well that all this enchantment would disappear with the coming of daylight, but I instantly threw this sober thought away and concentrated only on the moment. This moment was, for me, the only truth, and the only truth for me was that I loved him madly for what he was, although I knew that he was really... nothing.

No longer a princess and no longer the mistress, I fell down and embraced his legs.

"Please, Michael - I love you. Please stay. Do not leave me - not tonight."

He knelt down and took my face in his hands. Then he kissed me.

I kissed him back.

I took his hand and led him to the bedroom. We kissed again.

I took off his jacket. I undid his shirt, one button at a time and slid it over his arms.

I kissed his chest, his shoulders and his neck. I ran my hands over his hairy chest.

I kissed him again and undid his belt. Then his trousers. I let them drop to the floor.

I continued to kiss him and reached down and took his flaccid penis in my hand.

Whilst I did this, he just stood there, kissing me back.

I stopped. I took a step back, so he could see me, and stripped my sweater, then I took off my bra. Then I peeled off my trousers, leaving only my lacy thong on.

He just looked at me.

I took a step forward and kissed him hard.

He kissed me back, and we fell onto the bed.

I kissed his chest, I kissed his stomach, then I took his penis in my hand and kissed it, I licked it, and I took it in my mouth and sucked it.

Nothing happened.

I stopped and crawled up the bed, so I was level with him.

He put his arms around me, looked me in the eyes and kissed me.

I loved him. I only wanted to be close to him - to breathe his breath, smell his smell, and sleep with him, with his arms wrapped around me.

I fell asleep in his arms.

The night passed slowly.

Being unused to sleeping with anyone, his every movement woke me. His snoring woke me.

Sometimes he awoke when I touched him, and his snoring would stop. Then he would grab me and embrace me.

How happy I was... how tired I was.

Each time I awoke, I became more and more tired.

But at the time I did not mind.

Then morning came and I was exhausted. The love that I had felt was now bitterness at my lack of sleep. I could not look at him the same way I had the night before.

## CHAPTER THIRTY-TWO

It was a strange man I saw beside me when I awoke. In the glaring, morning sunlight I saw his wrinkles and the shadows under his eyes.

It was only seven a.m., but I was starving, since I had not eaten the previous day.

"Wait here," I said, after we had both dressed: "I'm going down to the garage to fetch my car."

"I don't want to go in your car," he said; "we have time to go by street-car."

"Why on Earth would I go by street-car?" I replied. "Besides, how would I return?"

"Call Nina: she'd pick you up on the moon, would she not?"

"I told you I cannot get hold of her."

"Of course," he nodded his head. "Well, I am travelling by street-car, so it is as to whether you join me."

I hated the street-car. I was already tired and irritable. The movement made me feel sick and it was starting to change the way I felt about

Michael - I blamed him for making me get on it.

The feeling of love I had for him the previous night had all but gone.

'But, Angelique,' I said to myself, 'you loved him so much last night. It can't disappear just like that, can it?'

I groped for his hand, yearning for the warmth it had given me so very recently. He pressed my hand, but I felt nothing.

We went to a little Chinese restaurant that was just opening up.

It was dreary. On this beautiful morning, the sunlight could hardly penetrate the dirty windows. The over-watered plant in the window had grown puny from lack of sunlight and Earth.

The restaurant was miserable, poor and dark, but I was so hungry I just ordered the first thing on the menu and ate it quickly. Afterwards, I felt much better. I looked at Michael, and the feeling of the night before started to return to me.

I was still tired though.

"I would like to go to your room."

He did not seem the least bit surprised - he did not try to persuade me to go to work. He just nodded.

Without speaking, we went out into the

sunlight again.

On our way to the subway station something strange happened: we passed a drugstore, and in the window, for some reason, was a male mannequin, with a rubber mask over his mouth.

"Isn't that funny?" he said.

I looked at it, and it disgusted me. I smiled outwardly, and said: "You are king of the masochists – that's what you are."

He laughed so loudly that the passers-by turned and stared at him. He couldn't stop laughing. With tears of laughter running down his cheeks, he jumped up and down, and danced like a madman, right in the middle of the street.

"The king!" he yelled; "I am the king!"

I was so glad when we arrived at his room. I went in and sat on his bed, whilst Michael went to get some water.

Michael's room was in one of those fine old sections of the city, where, inevitably, many of the elegant old mansions had been converted into bedsits. The room was very small but cosy.

As I waited for his return, I undressed. But with such a narrow space, I had to sit on the bed to take off my trousers.

I crawled into the bed. It felt so comfortable I just wanted to lie there forever and dream. What would he think if he returned and found me naked?

As I lay in bed I could not help but to think about Geoffrey: I thought of his body, his hard abs and chest. I thought about his bum and his penis.

I put my hand between my legs and felt myself. I was getting wet.

Then I thought about how Geoffrey had treated me. Damn! What a bastard he was. God, I hated him! Just like every other man in my life!

Then I thought about Michael. He is sweet. He has fallen on hard times, but he has this room, he has a job and he knows where he is going - he has ambition. I really admire him for this. I am sure that he just does not love me for a mistress: I think he loves me as a person, just like I admire him.

I was rubbing my pussy and thinking of Michael. I was getting more and more wet. The more I thought about Michael the more I wanted him.

The door clicked and Michael opened it.

He just stood there, staring at me in bed.

"Come on, Michael," I said.

He looked uneasy.

I crept across the bed, grabbed his shirt and pulled him towards me.

I began to kiss him.

He kissed me back.

I began tugging at his shirt to unbutton it. But he was not responding.

I undid his trousers and put my hand in his boxers and began to stroke his penis.

He was no longer kissing me

I wanted him to be erect for me. I wanted his manhood inside me and not just his tongue. He would be the third man I would have inside me.

I wanted him.

I knew deep down what I had to do.

"Come on," I said: "let me suffocate you."

Taken completely by surprise, he said: "You mean it? Right now?"

"Only if you undress, of course."

His nervous face relaxed into a smile and he began to undress.

I couldn't believe it had been that easy, or that difficult, to please him.

Michael took his shirt and trousers off, leaving just his boxers. Then he stood over the bed.

I got up and put my hand over his nose and kissed him.

My other hand went to his penis, and I felt his getting hard in my hand.

I pulled my head back, looked at him and

kissed him again. This time I put one hand on his nose and my other hand around his throat as I kissed him.

His pupils dilated.

I let go of his throat and began to rub his penis. I loved feeling of his erection growing in my hand.

I released my hand from his mouth but continue to kiss him and masturbate him.

"Tie me!" he moaned, when I allowed him a breath.

"No, I won't tie you."

"Tie me," he whimpered: "You are too weak - I will get away."

'You won't get away,' I thought – 'not now.'

I knew that he was not a good lover. But, still I needed him right now, and I knew what I had to do to get him. I took him by surprise so that he had no time to resist - I went around, grabbed him and pushed him down onto the bed. Then I straddled him.

I put my hand on my pussy and felt how wet I was. Then I took his penis in my hand and put him inside me.

Then I leant forward and gripped his neck with both my hands and squeezed.

I felt his erection grow even more inside me.

I looked at him in the eyes as I rode him.

"You see," I whispered: "you can do it without being tied. You could even do it without being suffocated, I bet."

"Does that give you a satisfying feeling of power? Power is the key to your character, isn't it Angelique? Power always has been and always will be your motivation for love, and you also find it a satisfactory substitute for love."

"Michael, stop talking. Come on: make love to me."

"Choke me harder, Angelique."

"No I won't," I replied; "not again. I want you to make love to me, as a man loves a woman, not as a slave worships a mistress."

I felt his penis begin to shrink inside me and with it any hopes I had of a relationship with Michael.

He stopped kissing and looked at me.

"I have fallen in love with you, Angelique, but I shall never put you in a gilded cage. I know I have only been in your life for a few months, so what right have I to step in at all? Yet, you told me that you loved me before I did! Last night, I didn't want to say it before I was certain, and yet I feared slighting you by not saying it. If you meant what you said about loving me, doesn't it give me some rights? At least the right to see you?"

"I loved you, Michael, at that particular moment," I said, "and at that particular moment, I really meant it."

"You declared your love for me, in or out of that damn fantasy world - what difference does it make? Do you really expect me to allow myself to become another slave? A puppet on a string, or a dog in a kennel?"

"I was *your* slave as well, and I am sure you won't forget that moment. *I* never will."

"Does an hour go by that you do not appear in my thoughts? Does a night pass that you do not possess my dreams? Does there come a dawn when you do not race the sun to my consciousness?"

"I won't forget the wonderful time we had, and, believe me, I felt real love for you."

"Don't turn this thing - which, for me, is a fragile and precious thing - into resentment, hate, and contempt, by the continuance of your dalliance."

"Please, Michael," I said. "We loved each other last night. Please."

But he did not listen. He pushed my arm away, and said sternly, almost viciously: "Power - this is the key to your character, so what is to be my role? Am I to have a role in your busy life? You always have so little time for what I say. For what catastrophic rainy day are you saving? Will you stifle love alive, and preserve it, like a stuffed animal, as a memorial of a conquest?"

"Michael, why do you mention power all the time as the key to my character? You are the one that cannot get an erection unless I am suffocating you."

"Such contemptuous words from such a despicable person. What really am I to you? How marvellous it must be to have me at your beck and call. Think of your marvellous apartment - which slave, I wonder, made this for you? And what slave do you entertain the most: *her*! Who and what am I to you? Am I slave number fifteen or lover number fifty-five? Do I just round out the wheel of phantom relationships, with which you have surrounded yourself? Slaves, lost loves, father figures..."

'Oh, God,' I thought: 'I should have never gone back to his apartment.' I never expected such an outbreak. I frantically searched for an answer. I started to tremble, and my heart fluttered.

He laughed hysterically and cried out: "Thank you, your majestic highness! Thank you! I kiss your foot." He flung himself on the bed and wept convulsively.

I was astonished, amazed, overwhelmed and

petrified. I sat up in bed, watching his
motionless form, and wondering what damage I
had done by loving him for those few days.
Then he flung his arms around me and buried
his head in my chest. I sat paralysed, unable to
caress him or comfort him with even a word.

"I am coming to realise that you stated a
very real truth when you lay in my arms and
whispered: 'You have a need for a great deal of
love, darling!' Oh, beloved, you were so right,
but I fear that the advantage you may take of it
will bury it suddenly. For years I have not really
felt alive, and now, for a few short days, I have
regained the knowledge of what life is about."

"So, you admit what I just said: you felt
really alive, and you regained the knowledge of
what life is about? So, remember the wonderful
time we had, and don't crucify me in that absurd
way, and annihilate everything we experienced."

"But Angelique, I can easily slide back into
the nether-world, and why should you care
unless you really do love me? Emotionally and
spiritually, that is what I feel tonight, Angelique,
because I cannot be with you forever. I am a key
without a lock, a star without a sky, a night
without a dawn… I am a flower in a gutter, a
song that was never sung, and an idea that was
never thought. I am all that was never needed,

and all that was discarded unused and unwanted. I am an Earth without rain or sun. I am a shoe that does not fit, a letter that was never sent… I am the seed that died."

'That is how *I* felt when I left Nice,' I thought.

That is *exactly* what I felt.

I felt immensely sorry for him, because I had gone through the precise emotions he now experienced. I had been discarded and unwanted, and so I had to leave my family and everything I had loved in my life.

He held my face in his hands, and with his tears dripping onto my breasts, he composed himself and spoke tenderly: "Perhaps this means nothing to you, but I think of you also in the tenderest thoughts. You have inspired me to write verse - something I have unsuccessfully attempted for years, because you have stirred in the depths of my being the latent poisons of fear, rejection, hate and death. I shall always remember the sweetest vision I have ever known, when I first glimpsed you in that brilliantly-lit instant. At that moment, I sensed eternity.

"I love you, my darling - passionately, jealously, and madly." Then, his voice trailed off into a whisper, with the words: "What is to be will be."

We lay silently together on the bed.

I knew that whatever it was I provided him when I was his mistress, I could not provide to him now, and I also knew that he could not give me what I needed. Deep down, without his submission, I meant little or nothing to him. I would disappear from his thoughts, and his love and admiration would simply transfer to the next mistress he found, whether it was Nina or someone else.

I felt his steady breath, as his limp body lay behind me, with his arms wrapped around me.

Although I really wasn't sorry for spending the last forty-eight hours with him, I cried silently, because I knew our relationship would go no further and I would be alone again.

## CHAPTER THIRTY-THREE

Michael's words continued to agitate me as I sat in my apartment, drinking gin and smoking cigarette after cigarette.

Many of the words he had spoken were true. Then my phone rang.

I cried when I heard her voice.

"What is wrong with you? What has happened, Angelique?" she said, surprised.

"Me?! What's wrong with me?! I have not spoken to you for over a week. I have been worried about you and missed you. And you ask me what is wrong with me?!"

"Of course Angelique, darling. I am fine. I know that Lisa has informed you that Richard's brother is unwell. However the situation is slightly more complicated."

"How do you mean?"

"When I tell you this I do not want you to worry more, for I am fine and out of danger. And I promise that you are also perfectly safe."

"Oh Nina, do tell me please."

"The vice police, of what I spoke about before, happened to visit my house. Luckily I was at my cottage at the time, so I was not caught..."

"Oh Nina! Please, please say it's not true. I am so worried."

"Angelique, I said do not worry. We are still in Calgary. I will be back soon. My lawyers are dealing with the police as we speak. I am very careful and have done nothing wrong, so there is no chance that anything further will come of this."

"Then how is it that they visited?"

"They most likely received false information from a begrudged former client and had to investigate. But I promise you there is nothing to worry about. Now tell me - have you been fooling around?"

"Is it obvious?" I asked.

"Of course - you sound like shit. Don't tell me you fooled around with a slave. Did I not warn you never to fool with a slave?"

"Yes, you did tell me not mess around and you said also that things can go wrong?" I replied. "Well, things went wrong - very wrong."

"With whom?"

"Michael."

There was a long silence, then she sighed. I heard her breathing down the phone, as if she was right next to me.

"I will be back soon Angelique, and I will see you. What will you do in the meantime?" she asked.

"I intend to move and disconnect my phone."

"This is a very wise idea," she said, in her deep and peaceful voice. "You sound exhausted - you really need to sleep. I left my pills in your bathroom last time I was there. Go and fetch them from the cabinet, take two of them, and you will sleep for at least twelve hours - you will wake a new person. Tomorrow we will work to relocate you, alight?"

I started to cry. "I love you, Nina. I love you more than anything in this world. You know this, right?"

"I know this, Angelique, and I will never, ever discard you the way you were discarded years ago in Nice. We will always be together. We will travel together, we will love together, and we will experience pain together. So be calm and take the pills. I will look after you, my darling."

"But why aren't you here with me now, when I need you?"

"Angelique, I would love nothing more than to be there with you now, but this is not to be. Take the pills and sleep, and when you sleep I will be next to you."

"Okay. Thank you, Nina. I love you."

"I love you too."

I pulled the phone cord out and went and took the pills.

I thought about Michael. I felt pity for him, and at the same time I felt guilt that I had given him a short period of pleasure, without being able to continue it. It was clear that whilst he may have thought he loved me, it was no more than an infatuation that he had to me, as his mistress. I doubt having been with the wife that left him for broke, for so long, enabled him to even know what love was, as I understood and needed it. But I could not be with him.

I thought about Nina. I loved her so much - more than I have ever loved any man.

I thought about Geoffrey. 'Oh, why can't Geoffrey be the man who loves me, like the man in the hotel loved me for the night?'

I felt sadness that I had been so hopelessly weak.

I felt the pills begin to take effect: I was very calm, quiet, and tranquil. All I had to do was seek Nina's advice.

Nina.

She always made me feel calm, quiet, and tranquil.

So did her pills.

I felt myself slipping into a hazy dream, where I would be happy.

## CHAPTER THIRTY-FOUR

I didn't wake up until three p.m. the next day. It took another hour for the fogginess in my mind to clear.

The pills had worked: I felt rested; I felt relaxed.

I looked around the apartment. The last thought I had had not been of Michael or Nina, but of Geoffrey.

Perhaps I had been too hard on him. I had to call him.

"Geoffrey, it's Angelique."

"I know - I can hear your voice. This is a most unexpected call."

"I want to see you again, Geoffrey. I want you to come round."

"Has Nina cast you away? Am I your second choice? Is that why you call me?"

"No, Geoffrey. It's not like that, and Nina would not cast me away. But I want to see you - I want to give you the session that you wanted."

"You already have, remember? Did the

money I left not speak well enough as to how satisfied I was with it?"

"It was *very* clear, Geoffrey," I said. "I mean a session with me - just me, without Nina."

"Now I know you have not spoken to Nina: such a request like this Nina would most certainly not approve. Whilst I know she speaks of the effort to get rid of me and to pass me to you, she is in no way eager to cut the strings from me yet and let me go. You are like a dog, and she tosses the scraps as to when she thinks you need them."

"Please don't speak about Nina like that."

"When do you want to have this session with me?"

"Tonight."

"That is too soon - you need to prepare yourself. Just like you and Nina prepared and planned the last one. "

"No, I mean it Geoffrey. Could you please come tonight?"

"No, Angelique. I cannot see you and will not see you tonight. I will see you tomorrow if my schedule permits me so."

This was the first time that Geoffrey said he could not meet me.

I held the phone in my hand after Geoffrey had hung up. Then I drank gin and tonic and smoked.

I waited all day for Geoffrey to call, to see if he would see me that night. He phoned me eventually at one o'clock, and told me that he would be at my apartment at seven that evening.

I spent the rest of the day getting ready.

I tidied the apartment and lay out all of the things that I had: a long, thick, braided rope, my bull-whip, my riding crop, my lash, ankle and wrist cuffs, chains and a belt.

I went to my wardrobe and put on my skin-tight black leather corselet and knee-high black leather boots.

Then I waited for the knock on my door.

The heels on my knee-length boots banged against the wooden floor with each step.

When I answered, he smiled. But his smile had now lost its softness - I saw sharp lines around his mouth, but when he embraced me, the lines faded. His entire physique was that of an exquisite man.

I invited him in and told him to sit down. He had a scent that I found overwhelmingly sexy - this scent belonged to Geoffrey and *only* to him.

"Are you going to beat me really hard this Time, now that Nina isn't here to help you?"

"Please stop talking about Nina."

Geoffrey didn't reply, but just sat there staring at me.

"Tie me," he said.

"Later, Geoffrey. Why don't we go out like before? Remember when you took me out and treated me like a princess? I had such an amazing time."

"Yes it was a fantastic time, especially for you. But I am not here for that now. You promised me a session - that is the only reason I came round. I can leave if you wish, and we can go out another time."

"Don't leave. You will have your session. I just thought we could talk first. I love the way you talk."

Geoffrey got up off the sofa reached for his jacket.

"No!" I said, standing in front of Geoffrey. I put my hand on his broad chest. "Come on – let's do this session."

Geoffrey just looked at me with cold eyes - I could see no warmth in them for me at all, and it broke my heart.

"Tie me," he said, as he began undressing. This time it did nothing for me to see his naked body.

I took the rope, wrapped it tightly around

his body and tied it into a knot.

I looked down at him on the floor, at my feet. I no longer felt the same power I used to - I just felt pity for him.

"Lead me around the room like a dog."

I took the rope and pulled him round. He crawled easily. I wasn't sure who was more humiliated by this - me or Geoffrey.

Then I stopped.

"Kick me," he said. "

'God, he really is crazy.' If I had felt angry at Geoffrey, I would have thought that this would have been easy for me. But I just felt empty. I didn't want to do any of it.

"With the stiletto heel of your foot."

I looked at him and shook my head. Then I kicked him anyway. The heel dug in and the skin on his thing immediately bruised, and started bleeding.

"Beat me, Angelique. Beat me hard."

I went and got the riding crop.

I hit Geoffrey with it.

"Is that it? Is that all you have Angelique? Perhaps you are useless."

I hit him again, harder.

He stared up at me; "Pathetic."

I hit him again.

I took the riding crop in one hand and the

bull-whip in the other. And I just hit him with both.

Geoffrey sat on the floor as I beat him.

Red welts showed up all over his body.

I untied the rope.

Then he looked up at me; "Choke me."

I wrapped it around his neck. 'If he really wants me to choke him, I will.'

I held his face with one hand, kissed him and pulled the rope with the other.

His face started to get blue as he struggled helplessly.

He struggled more and more.

I pulled tighter.

His eyes were bugling. His face turned bright red, then blue.

I saw his erection grow.

I pulled tighter, until I heard a strange sound coming from his throat.

Then I let go and unwound the rope.

Geoffrey collapsed to the floor.

"Now, Geoffrey," I said; "You got your satisfaction, didn't you?"

Geoffrey was on the floor, on his hands and knees, panting. After several minutes he looked up. "Yes," he smiled: "I really got my satisfaction."

I released his bonds.

I pitied him in a way, but yet I realised that I too had acted like an animal. When I had calmed myself a little, I began to wonder what it would be like to suffer this myself.

"Now tie me and try it on me," I said, softly.

"What?"

"Tie me. I want you to tie me. I want to know - I want to understand. I love you, Geoffrey. I don't know how you can do this, but I want to know. I want to understand."

"Somehow, I knew that you would ask this," he replied; "I was just waiting for it."

"Really? Well, then what are you waiting for."

Geoffrey took the rope and began wrapping it around my body. Then he tied it and looked down at me.

Terror gripped me, but I hoped that he would never hurt me.

I didn't understand it. I didn't feel what he obviously felt.

I looked at him and shook my head. "Chain me on the bar," I said.

Geoffrey undid the rope, took my legs and chained me, spread-eagled. I felt like a bird with clipped wings. As I waited for the first blow my terror was indescribable.

I felt so exposed. I could not believe how

many times I had done this to other slaves. I knew what it felt like now: I felt exposed and vulnerable. I needed to understand more.

"The whip - use the small whip, please, Geoffrey."

Geoffrey sneered and picked up the whip.

I awaited the first blow. I began to sweat - I felt it running down my body. I was scared. I am sure Geoffrey was deliberately delaying.

"Come on, Geoffrey. Just do it, please."

I couldn't see him - he was behind me. I began to get scared.

*Whack.*

The first whack just shocked me.

I let out a cry.

The he hit me again. And again. Five times in total.

By the end I was crying. I still didn't understand the feeling though.

I heard myself saying: "Take the tougher one and lash me harder."

He replied with five strokes that cut my skin like a sword.

Imagining the welts on my back and buttocks, my mind was a captive of the situation, and my lips kept repeating: "Harder. Harder. Harder! Hurt me!"

Geoffrey finally stopped whipping me, and

undid my chains.

I recovered quickly, but still did not understand. I needed to understand.

"Now suffocate me," I begged.

Without a word, Geoffrey sat on my chest.

I was nervous as he reached down and put his hands around my throat. My neck felt so small in his hands.

He began to squeeze.

First of all I felt the pressure on the front of my neck, then it travelled round my neck.

It got tighter.

I tried to tuck my head down to try and allow myself to breathe.

His hands got tighter.

I looked up at his face.

Very quickly, I felt the pressure building in my throat, and then I felt the pressure in my head, in my face and my eyes.

He had this strange, forced smile on his face. I could not tell if he was enjoying it or not.

My head began to hurt.

Then the pressure spread to my face and eyes.

I began to panic.

I tried to speak, but couldn't get words out.

My hands were too heavy to lift - they barely touched his arms.

I began to struggle wildly, to try and break his grip.

I couldn't even see if he was smiling any more.

I couldn't see anything.

Then, a rush of air.

I opened my eyes and felt light-headed, like I had been spinning around on the spot, and had fallen down.

This was so much worse than the chains or the whip, but I could not speak or beg for air.

I struggled so wildly that he released me, and I collapsed.

I lay on the floor, getting my air back.

"Geoffrey, this is terrible," I whimpered. "This is unbelievable! It is beyond description - you are crazy, nuts and sick… sick!"

Geoffrey stared at me, then shouted: "You are the one who enjoys having the power over me - a power that you would not have if I did not allow it. I don't know why I need it, any more than you know why such domination is an ingrained bit of your psyche."

"I don't believe that I could ever inflict this on anybody now that I have experienced it, because I will always feel the sickness you have just imposed on me!" I shrieked.

"Hypocrite!" he shouted: "such nonsense

you speak! You forget, I am the one that looked into your soul and showed it to you, with a gift that only a god could make: the mirrored box that I handed to you when you truly were a princess, but lost before your discovery of your need for power, and my submission. You need this, Angelique, as much as any slave."

"You speak too much Geoffrey, and you think too little, except of yourself. Whilst you gave me the mirrored box, it was Nina that found and showed me my soul, and now she is not here!"

"The sampled and satiated fruit, Nina - the forbidden fruit to come; the other love princess!" he screamed. "Send you the cast-offs - how many do you have? Fifteen or fifty-five slaves? You have the power over such men, and you use it to search for your lost lovers and father figures!"

"And they want that!" I shrieked. "They are lining up in front of my door, you fool. Have I forced anybody to do anything? I have only provided what they apparently need, and especially you, Geoffrey. You evidently need it to live!"

His eyes grew wide and his body began to shake.

"I had such fondness and devotion to you.

Now I just have hatred and contempt!" he spat. "I think of Aeneas' journey into the darkness of the Styx. That's what you do to me!" he screamed at me.

'For goodness' sake,' I thought, 'what on Earth does *"Aeneas, the journey into the darkness of the Styx"* mean? It must be something really bad.' Whilst I was contemplating his words, Geoffrey dressed.

"So I won't see you again, Geoffrey. I bid you well for your cruise. Why don't you take this with you? If you meet another princess you can woo her with it."

I picked up the mirrored box and dropped it at his feet.

The glass in it shattered, then the sides split open and tiny fragments of glass erupted across my apartment floor.

"That is what your soul looks like, Angelique. When Nina contacts you again, ask her to pick it up for you."

With that. Geoffrey stormed out of the flat and slammed the door shut.

I went and sat on the sofa and cried.

## EPILOGUE

It was another two weeks before Nina was able to return from Calgary.

She came straight to my apartment from the airport and didn't even go home first. When I saw her, I ran to her arms, embraced her and wept.

I realised that although I loved Nina, she only loved me - and *could* only love me - as a friend. She had her husband, and she could never love me in the way that I needed.

Nina would always remain my friend and soulmate - someone that I would trust with my life, and someone I could call upon any time.

But I knew I had to move on and start the next chapter of my life.

I had already been offered a job at a one of Canada's largest companies - I decided that I would take the job and work as hard as I could. At the same time, I would study. I was determined to rise to the top.

I had to leave the apartment, so Nina helped

me dismantle the flat's "bizarre" set-up, as Michael had called it - it needed to be ready for the building superintendent to inspect.

When he arrived, he was very nice, and told me he was very sorry that I had to leave, and that he would miss having such a fantastic tenant.

I thought about the men in my life.

Michael did believe that he loved me, and I could have loved him. But the truth was that he worshipped me, and was infatuated by me more as a mistress, then as a person.

The same with Geoffrey: I did love Geoffrey, and I wanted him to love me as much. But he did not want it - not friendship, not affection, and not my love. He wanted no friends. He would make no sacrifice for anyone.

After I experienced what each of my slaves asked me to put them through, I realised I could do this no more.

All of my other slaves - Rod, Keith and Peter - went back to Nina.

My new apartment was in the West End of Toronto, close to the airport and close to Nina's house. I also had a beautiful white convertible. Because it was close to Nina's house, I still saw her regularly, but I never saw her whip another slave.

When I got my new telephone number I called my parents. I gave them my new number, my new address, and even my phone number at work. I told them about my promotion and that I had passed my university courses.

The first phone call I received was from my sister. After we spoke about ourselves, she told me about Damien: he was now married, but they could not have children. After several medical tests on the wife came back clear, it became apparent that it was *he* who had a genetic condition which meant he could not have children.

How did I feel about this?

I felt nothing. Damien had rejected me for his own fault, but still I could not bear him any ill will, as I had already, in the two years since, had more of a life than I ever would have done with him.

## ACKNOWLEDGEMENTS

The author would like to thank her husband Ben for his love and support.

The publisher would like to thank Matt Vidler and Russell Spencer for their hard work and dedication in getting this book published.

The author and publisher would like to thank pixabay.com and canva.com for their help and assistance with the cover.

## ABOUT THE AUTHOR

Angelique Manon is a French-Canadian author and the retired Vice President of one of Canada's largest Fortune 500 companies.

She is author of *"Angelique - Femme Fatale"* and *"The Mirrored Box"*.

She lives with her husband in Ontario, and enjoys seeing her children and old friends.

Angelique loves to hear from her readers, and can be contacted at: angelique.manon@vianet.ca

## ABOUT THE PUBLISHER

L.R. Price Publications is dedicated to publishing books by unknown authors.

We use a mixture of both traditional and modern publishing options to bring our authors' words to the wider world.

If you are, an author interested in getting your book published, or a book retailer interested in selling our books, please contact us.

www.lrpricepublications.com

L.R. Price Publications Ltd,
27 Old Gloucester Street, London,  WC1N 3AX.

(020) 8144 9188

publishing@lrprice.com